DESCENT INTO HELL

A MODERN REIMAGINING OF DANTE'S INFERNO

SAMUEL FLEMING

Thank you to my Beta Readers

and to my First Reader,

Mel.

Contents

Base of Operations

Dr. David Levy

"Come on. What's going on out there?"

"Trust me, sir. You don't want to see." Not that there were any windows.

David Levy shifted nervously in his seat in the back of the army truck. He was the only civilian. Quietly sitting and clad in jeans and a brown polo. The other ten wore a mix of camouflage uniforms and talked casually amongst themselves. Even though he'd trimmed his hair and beard, he felt scraggly in comparison to the crew cuts and clean faces.

They were driving through some undisclosed location in the Middle East. He'd flown in on two puddle jumpers and then driven through several small towns. It had been three hours since he'd heard anything outside resembling a town. David wasn't at liberty to know more about the location or the nature of his work, only that he would be translating for the U.S. Army.

Every few minutes a whisper would pass by the truck and everyone would stop talking. It wasn't the sound of conversation or a market. It was the sound of someone whispering incoherently, almost hissing, and moving quickly around the moving truck from one side to the other, with the speed of a bird circling.

The soldiers said it was ghosts. Some shuddered at the sounds outside and the rest went back to nervous conversation.

Hours later the transport truck came to a stop. The back of the truck opened up into a building instead of open air. David followed the soldiers as they hopped out. Then a tall, dark-haired woman in uniform with dark hair greeted them. She called names off a clipboard and told them where they were to report to.

David listened for his name and looked around. The structure they were in was a temporary structure, a glorified tent made of metal bones and canvas skin, but they were surprisingly effective. He knew this because he had a previous, though brief, stint translating for the Army in the Middle East. The colors of sunset were starting to show through the cream colored canvas. It was warm, at least eighty degrees, but not the sweltering hundred degrees that David had braced himself for.

Behind him, there was just enough of a gap between the transport truck and the fabric opening of the tent to see a little beyond. David stared. Outside was green… Grass and trees. He hadn't seen anything like that in his time in Nawadin.

Then a figure walked between the trees in the distance—no, it glided. It was silvery and moved with inhuman smoothness over the roots and rocks. Then it was gone.

Another glimpse of a wispy figure.

David walked toward the back of the truck, toward the gap. Hypnotized and in a cold sweat.

A hissing whisper came from somewhere outside and made David shiver. What were those things? They couldn't be… They had to be some kind of holographic technology designed to scare people, to keep them out of the compound. The hissing grew louder with every second that his eyes lingered.

"Dr. David Levy," said a woman's voice from behind him.

He whipped around, startled and somewhat embarrassed. "Yes, sir—ma'am."

The woman with the clipboard. A hint of a smile. "They don't like it when you stare."

"They—they?"

"The ghosts," she said flatly. "They don't like it when you stare. I'm Captain Miller. Come with me, please."

Dr. David Levy followed Captain Miller through the maze of canvas and steel that was this impromptu military base. David had guessed wrong. Initially he had thought she was a lieutenant from the two silver bars on her uniform. He never could keep military ranks straight, even after his first time translating. He just remembered enlisted had rows, officers had bars and the "brass" had clovers and birds. Stars for generals.

"How much do you know?" she asked.

David shrugged, not that she could see it—he was walking behind her after all. "Not much. I'm a translator. I'm going to be translating. They told me that I was in the Middle East. They said they needed someone who knew Hebrew, Greek, and Latin; which I thought was odd but they weren't exactly forthcoming with my questions."

"They told you enough," she said. "You'll hear more at the briefing, but the rest you'll have to see for yourself."

They walked briskly through a large hanger that had been cut into several paths with canvas screens. These divided rooms and hallways were packed with all manner of soldiers and officers, all of them busy. It was like a small city.

David tried wrapping his head around the scale, but he had very little context for what military operations looked like. The other time he worked for the Army he supported a small team in the lowland town of Nawadin and the two military bases were incomparable. The operation there consisted of two buildings and a tent.

Whatever was going on here was orders of magnitude bigger.

After dozens of twists and turns, they stopped at a small alcove stacked with textbooks. A stocky, middle aged woman with frizzy blond hair sat hunched over one of the books. In the bustle of the military base she hadn't heard them approach.

The young officer cleared her throat. "Dr. Reed, this is Dr. Levy."

The frizzled Dr. Reed turned in her chair and smiled widely. "Please, call me Nancy."

"*The* Dr. Nancy Reed?" David asked. She nodded. "Oh wow. Your papers on the transition from biblical Greek to Latin were one of the foundations of my thesis."

From her chair, Nancy waved her hands in a bow. "Well thank you David."

To the side, the young captain smiled again. "I'll leave you two. Someone will come get you for the briefing at 1900." She turned and left before David could reply.

"They do that here," Nancy said with a shrug. "Here. Sit, sit." She moved a colorful stack of textbooks off of a chair and set them on the plastic floor. "You must be the one they brought in to translate Hebrew."

"I guess so. If they brought you on then they certainly don't need me for Greek or Latin." David sat down in the folding chair and could almost pretend that he was back in one of the offices at his college. From somewhere in the alcove he caught a whiff of cedar.

He regarded his colleague. She was not at all what he expected. In order to be considered to accompany military operations, civilians had to pass a physical fitness test. It wasn't an insurmountable bar—David had passed the test with three workouts a week and a potbelly—but the test had humbled him. He passed the run with fifteen seconds to spare. He had assumed that his idol was an old, out of shape professor (which seemed to be becoming the standard back home). Dr. Reed was lean and as broad through the shoulders as he was and he imagined her having an easier time with the fitness test as well.

David shook his head and then went on, "The longer I'm here the more I realize just how little they told me. I didn't even know that they would have other translators. What did they tell you?"

"I imagine I know about as much as you." She gestured as she spoke. "I think they found something. Whatever it is, it's old enough that they needed translators that were fluent in three of the oldest languages to help them."

David's excitement of meeting one of his idols was fading already and his thoughts drifted back to the ghosts that he saw outside.

He started to ask, "Did you see—"

Dr. Reed nodded. "They weren't exactly forthcoming with those details, but I did overhear a little bit." She leaned in to whisper. "They refer to them as *spectral anomalies*. The soldiers just call them ghosts. They're mostly harmless."

"*Mostly?*"

Her whisper turned somber. "They lost some soldiers when the forest was first discovered. The soldiers have orders not to engage them. The casualties stopped when the soldiers quit engaging and the scientists stopped studying them. That's why they won't let *us* study the ghosts. Not that I want to study them."

"You know what, I'm okay with that. Ghosts are already more than I signed up for."

They both chuckled nervously, a sentiment which quickly faded.

David said, "Christ, instead of studying ghosts outside, everyone's in here... What did they find? What are we doing here?"

This time, Dr. Reed didn't even shrug. "I don't know. I don't know."

At 7:00 pm, two soldiers came to escort the two translators through the bustling hallways and a narrow connecting tent to a large secondary room. The room was large and open. At the front was a projector and screen.

In the middle of the room were two dozen folding chairs. A dozen soldiers sat in half of the chairs on the far side of the room. Most of them had lap desks with notebooks, wore T-shirts instead of the full fatigues the other soldiers wore. They also hadn't shaved, which was odd. Didn't all soldiers have to shave?

All of their heads turned to see who approached.

Nancy waved sheepishly, "Just your translators."

Some of the men nodded, but they all turned back to the front.

The two civilians quietly took the closest empty seats. David fought the urge to study the soldiers, if only to take his mind off his nervousness. He assumed they were army, but couldn't tell from a cursory glance.

Captain Miller stood at the front of the room with her clipboard. She called attention a moment later for the Commanding Officer when he walked in—David almost stood out of reflex. Colonel Jensen was tall with sharp, dark features. He called, "at ease", and they both settled in at the front for the briefing.

Colonel Jensen started clicking through a presentation while he talked. "The forest we are situated in appeared sometime in the last four years. To date, no locals can tell us exactly when it appeared and our satellite intel is limited. Three years ago, local farmers stumbled into these woods. We're told that at that time there were no spectral anomalies in the forest. Some months afterward, some of those same locals discovered a cavern with ancient architecture. This location was brought to our attention last year and we've since set up this forward base to study the many anomalies present."

He clicked through several slides showing a thin entryway that opened up into a cavern that couldn't have been bigger than the briefing room they were in now. At the back of the cavern was an ornately carved archway with two doors. Some of the lettering was definitely Greek and others might have been Hebrew. Both David and Nancy leaned forward but shook their heads; the pictures weren't close enough for David to read the writing.

The Colonel smiled. "Don't worry. You're going there at 0500 tomorrow."

Captain Miller clasped her hands behind her back and continued the briefing. "Forward teams have already set up two staging areas inside different sections of the cavern. You will convene with them, resupply and receive further briefings. Radio communication between Home Base and the Staging Areas is limited so they'll be best able to brief you with changing conditions.

"The caverns inside are varying sizes. Some are wide enough for an entire company of soldiers to get lost in. Others will require single file movement." The slideshow clicked forward through several different caverns, including a massive cavern with a river cutting through it.

The Colonel said, "Inside you will encounter more spectral anomalies." Several slides flashed of ghostly creatures, all human-like save for their transparent skin and clothes. Then several slides of normal looking people with various wounds and sores. Then several more slides of very normal-looking people in all manner of clothes: Robes, Victorian era dress, modern suits, native loincloths.

"Some of them are intelligent and, in spite of their appearances, many of them are benign. It's thought that they're related to the spectral anomalies that now inhabit the woods around the cavern. Once again, you will receive further briefing from the Staging Areas. Do not engage unless absolutely necessary.

"Your translators, Dr. David Levy and Dr. Nancy Reed, will assist you with any communication or translation needs you have.

"Virgil will be your guide from here until Staging Area Bravo. Heed his word down below and you'll make it at least to the second Staging Area. He is en route from Staging Area Alpha and will be here for your 0500 departure.

"Your objectives are to explore and infiltrate to each Staging Areas and beyond. We don't know how deep the cavern goes, but your orders are to go as deep as possible and report back what you find."

Captain Miller added, "If you have any questions, now is the time."

David's mouth was still hanging open.

One of the soldiers asked in a Southern accent, "How can we identify which ones are hostile?"

The Captain replied, "That's a question for the Staging Areas. You shouldn't encounter any resistance until you get past Staging Area Alpha."

Beside him, Nancy was in silent awe. So David raised his hand. "Forgive me if this is out of place, but where are the scientists? We've made contact with ghosts or—ah, spectral anomalies... Where is the research party?"

This time the Captain looked to the Colonel. He replied, "We currently have scientists and research teams inside the cavern, but they are being kept to the outer portions for safety reasons. The Staging Areas will brief you further."

David wasn't satisfied with that answer, but when he glanced around the room, all eyes were on the Colonel. "And they speak Hebrew, Greek or Latin?" David asked.

"Correct. I understand that this is surprising to you, Dr. Levy. I cannot answer all the particulars about their forces. I suggest you make a list of questions for the Staging Areas when you arrive."

David shrank down in his chair. The whole thing wasn't sitting right with him. Why quarantine the scientists to the outer caverns? Why send in soldiers and translators?

Unless the things—people—in the inner cavern were hostile.

"Dr. Levy and Dr. Reed, you're dismissed. I suggest you get some shut eye. You have a long trek tomorrow," Captain Miller said.

~

Lieutenant Hector Ramirez

The lieutenant watched the translators leave.

When he was with the Rangers, seeing a civilian on the squad was a rare occurrence; so rare that the squad would try to guess all manner of things about them. It was a game back then or maybe like a divided middle school dance: Rangers on one side, civilians on another. Then when he was on Delta Force, the squads used to joke with the academics. They still wouldn't go out of their way to fraternize, but it was more like high school—neither party minded the attention.

His time on Omega Squad was different. Now they worked with academics on every mission—at least a dozen different ones. The novelty of working with civilians was long gone. Everyone had a job to do and the civilians that tagged along were good about doing theirs too.

Once the translators were gone, the rest of the mission briefing began.

Colonel Jensen clasped and unclasped his hands behind his back several times before starting. Not surprising. Most higher ups—most normal people—were shaken when they found things that were worth calling Omega for.

The Colonel said, "I understand that you were told a number of things about this mission. I also understand that most of you have been with Omega long enough to read between the lines—to know what's bullshit and what you can take to the bank.

"I meant what I said in the original briefing: We are still processing this situation. There are a lot of unknowns. Your main directives are the same: Do not engage unless attacked.

Make it to Staging Area Alpha and then to Bravo and then see how deep the rabbit hole goes. Questions?"

This time the lieutenant's second-in-command spoke up, Non-Commissioned Officer, Sergeant Wilson. "Sir, have they decided on a name for what we're dealing with?"

Ramirez almost smiled—that was Wilson's way of trying to get just a little more information out of the ranking officer. When it came to situations like these—situations where Omega is called in—the ranking officer never wanted to say anything that they haven't been cleared to say.

That meant no talking of ghosts, spirits, mutants, aliens, demons—no talk of the occult. And the occult was exactly what Omega specialized in.

The Colonel pursed his lips. "The brass are hesitant to label anything you're about to see or encounter. No doubt you'll hear rumors. Take them with a grain of salt."

He waited another moment for questions, and then dismissed himself. The Colonel walked away briskly. He seemed shaken about what was happening here, but then Lieutenant Ramirez had seen worse.

Hopefully the Captain would be more forthcoming. Worst case, Omega would mingle with the base and find whatever rumors they could. In their line of work, rumors were often better than intel.

Captain Miller dismissed them. When the squad looked to him, Lieutenant repeated her dismissal for the evening. They were to report for outfitting at 0400 tomorrow morning.

Both Ramirez and Sergeant Wilson lingered behind with Miller. When they were alone, Ramirez asked, "What do you think of all this, Captain?"

She sighed and looked at the canvas—through the canvas—searching for something to say. "I'm not at liberty to say."

"I understand that, ma'am. I'm just curious about your opinion. Not your analysis."

The captain shook her head. "You don't understand, Lieutenant. I'm really not at liberty to say."

Lieutenant Ramirez and Sergeant Wilson walked through the bustling military complex, going nowhere in particular. Ramirez was disappointed at the captain's answer, but it wasn't wholly unexpected; she was one of the brass, after all.

Eventually the two of them would find the mess hall, but for now, they enjoyed being two normal-ish soldiers in a top secret base. That was one of the things that most civilians got wrong about special forces: If you lined up twenty soldiers without insignia and asked them to pick out the special forces, they would get it wrong every time. Special Operations (spec ops, for short) didn't look any different from any other enlisted soldiers. They weren't taller, shorter, or have bigger muscles or any other obvious tells.

Actually, there was one tell: If you caught spec ops between quick deployments, you would find they were the only soldiers on base that weren't clean shaven or that could get away with wearing a half-assed uniform. That was one of the perks to an otherwise miserable, violent, and thankless existence. When you could do the things that spec ops soldiers did—and do them quietly—the brass cut you more slack than the average soldiers.

And most didn't boast about what squad they were in. In Ramirez's experience, the spec ps that boasted at the bar were either fresh cut or outright liars.

But all that didn't mean that special forces couldn't recognize each other; there was always *the look*. It might be choosing to sit with their back to the wall, eyes on the entrances to a room. Other times it might be the ease with which they sat, comfortable knowing exactly what to do should *any* situation arise. Sometimes it was just their eyes; looking at someone and knowing that they had seen some shit.

Ramirez hadn't quite figured that last one out yet, but it was true. Sometimes just looking into the eyes of another soldier was enough sometimes. The personal academic in Ramirez thought that combat left an imprint on people. Spec Ops just saw more combat than the average soldier. Call it pain or trauma—Ramirez never quite delved that far into it. He preferred to think of it like a mistake on a stone carving.

That was why he had seen *the look* in old combat vets. No matter how distant the memories, the imprint was still there. It would always be there. The stone would always have that gouge in it.

Ramirez and Wilson walked through two more passages. On the way they passed soldiers from Omega, some even mingled with other enlisted from the base.

Turner, Harris and Lee sat together against an open bench in the cafeteria. They were enthusiastically passing their phones to one another, probably sharing pictures of their latest conquests. It had become a ritual that the Lieutenant disdained.

They passed Davis and Gomez cleaning their M4's by the armory. Their guns were dismantled and laid out neatly on the table. Their knives were out as well. Davis's sniper rifle was wrapped in white cloth and lay on the table beside him; it would have been the first thing he cleaned and oiled. All of it was standard ritual for two men brought together by violence—both their skill and the ease with which it came to them.

They finally came to an open building—the rec area. Inside a dozen soldiers were playing basketball on a makeshift court. Two games of cornhole were on the far side. On the right side, a dozen more enlisted sat on benches, talking and watching the games. Kim, one of Omega Squad, sat with the regulars and watched the game. In the far corner, Smith sat around a card table with other soldiers from the base. He was quiet and concentrating, which usually meant he was winning.

Ramirez and Wilson took a seat on the bleachers, nodding at the nearby soldiers. Out here the two weren't Officer and Sergeant. Out here, the two were friends of ten years, just killing time like the rest of the men and women.

"What do you make of it?" Wilson asked.

Ramirez shook his head. "They've got a mix of spirits and… flesh curses, maybe."

"Walkers?"

Ramirez nodded. "Could be voodoo, but that doesn't fit with the languages."

"I don't like it," Wilson added.

"You never do."

Wilson rolled his eyes. "You know what I mean. Usually the brass is quick to label stuff like this—the brass or the scientists are. Why haven't they categorized the creatures or given this place a name?"

Ramirez looked around at the enlisted soldiers enjoying their leisure, wondering what it would be like to be as blissfully ignorant as them.

It was likely the Colonel and the Captain didn't fully understand what was happening here. The real Commanding Officer was likely at one of the Staging Areas—that was why the Colonel kept deferring.

Ramirez sighed. "The brass doesn't want to put a name on what they've found. Whatever it is, it's big and probably biblical. They'll throw around other religions and monsters all day long, but the brass doesn't like labeling demons and angels and nephilim."

"Shit…" Wilson muttered.

"Yep."

The men of Omega were the best of the best, handpicked from other spec ops teams, across branches and across the allied nations—but it wasn't work that most readily signed up for. By definition, most of Omega's work was existential and deadly. Their casualty rate was triple any other special forces' numbers. This meant most soldiers didn't stick around for more than a few deployments—they didn't want to keep rolling the dice.

They were called in for the things that couldn't be explained by normal means and that couldn't be contained by normal means. The supernatural was their specialty. And Lieutenant Ramirez and Sergeant Wilson had seen about all the different things there were to see: Vengeful spirits, voodoo zombies, dream-eating baku, plague-mutated creatures, science experiments gone wrong. Even the biblical: Angels, demons and nephilim.

Biblical missions were the worst. Most of that high casualty rate came from those missions.

That wasn't because they were the most dangerous, but because they were the most existential. Filling a zombie, vampire or spirit full of magic-laced bullets was something they could all do and then sleep soundly at night. The real challenge was confronting demons that really could lurk in your closet, ancient beings (the nephilim) were just as corrupt as humans, and, of the three, angels were by far the scariest. There was no telling what would land you on the wrong side of them. Other creatures might see the world morally in black and white, or in shades of gray. Angels saw it somewhere between blue and orange, and it was all too easy to find yourself on the wrong side of one.

Most soldiers can live with shooting and killing someone else's god, but not their own. Most people can live with knowing that there is some truth to all the world's legends and religions, but most have a hard time living after they realize just how little they matter in the grand scheme—even to their own god.

The pair sat for a bit and watched the games, taking part of a bit of normalcy. At one point Wilson got up to play a game of basketball, but not Ramirez—he never played.

It wasn't out of disdain for the regular enlisted; he wouldn't play with his own squad or with officers either. He just didn't play games. It was like dancing—he didn't do that either. Some people thought he was a stick in the mud. His wife Tracey had called him that early on when they were dating but she thankfully had left it behind now that they were married.

A part of him knew it went back to his wallflower days in grade school, but Ramirez didn't want to analyze it further than that. So Ramirez watched the game, cheering and heckling both teams.

It was a close game—Wilson's team lost by three points.

Afterward, Wilson sat back down on the bench with Ramirez while another round of fresh players started a game.

"You went easy on them," Ramirez said. "You could have outrun all those guys."

Wilson shrugged, breathing easy. "Maybe. Guess I got the mission on my mind."

"Something. Come on, let's get some chow," Ramirez offered a hand to his friend.

"Shit, I just sat down."

"You can rest when you're dead."

Reluctantly, Wilson took Ramirez's hand and allowed himself to be pulled to his feet. The two walked off toward the mess hall, talking over each other's shoulders as they squeezed single file between dividers and people.

"Did you call Tracey yet?" Wilson asked.

"I called her yesterday."

"Yeah but we're going in tomorrow. Probably won't get the chance to call for a while."

Ramirez turned and joked to his friend, "You probably just want me to put you on the phone with her. Not a chance!"

Wilson cracked a smile but pressed on, "I just have a bad feeling about this one. You sure you aren't going to call them?"

"No," Ramirez shook his head. "I talked to Tracey and Anna yesterday. Tracey knows how much I love her. They know."

"Alright then," Wilson said with a shrug. "I'm going to call home after chow. Let the folks know that I'll be gone."

"That's good. Your mom always was a sweetheart—

"Hey now!"

So it went. When they weren't CO and Sergeant, Hector Ramirez and Atticus Wilson were best friends. They met in basic training and had been friends even before Hector had met his now wife, Tracey.

The Army was one of the best things to happen to Ramirez. The other three were Atticus, Tracey and Anna. The order depended upon who was asking: Tracey and Anna were always tied for the best—except when Tracey asked Hector what was the best thing to happen to him. Then Ramirez's answer depended on how playful he felt like being.

If Tracey was his soulmate, then Atticus was Ramirez's squadmate. Complements to one another: Ramirez was the wallflower, Wilson was eager to act. Ramirez was better at planning, Wilson at improvisation. They had even grown up in neighboring counties on the West Coast.

The two were inseparable through their time in the service, and were lucky enough to come up together through the ranks. Both had been destined for special forces and gifted enough to be considered for Delta Force and finally Omega Squad. Somehow they hadn't tired of each other after ten years.

Every time they were back home from deployment, Atticus would spend a day or two with the Ramirezes and felt like he was a part of the family.

After chow, the two went to the barracks tent, again connected through canvassed hallways. On the way they passed a designated smoking tent with fans and a vent in the ceiling of the canvas. Absolutely no one was allowed outside.

There were only a few enlisted smoking. On the far side, Miller was talking on his sat-phone. Ramirez only heard one word loud enough to make out: *Bitch*. Probably his wife.

Ramirez shook his head. Half his squad probably shouldn't have those damn things, even if they were base-approved.

Wilson said, "Come on. You don't make it into Omega without having serious problems."

Ramirez shrugged. He couldn't deny that most of his squad had issues. Clark and Kim seemed alright enough. So did his best friend. Those weren't good odds. Ramirez supposed he had a few too, but he hadn't sat with himself long enough to admit them. He didn't get to be picky with the men that served in his unit. Maybe that was why the saying, *I trust you with my life, but not my money or my wife,* came from.

The barracks was one of the larger tents, lined with rows and rows of bunks. The night shift were still sleeping in many of the bunks even though their duty hour was fast approaching.

In the far side of the room, Young was laying in his bunk, endlessly scrolling through his phone. He'd been that way for a while now: Quiet and kept to himself. He spent most of his free time on his phone. Of all the vices one could have, Ramirez supposed it wasn't that bad.

Ramirez kicked off his boots and hopped up on his designated bunk.

"I'm going to call the folks," Wilson said, gesturing with his sat-phone for emphasis. "Be in the smoking section."

Ramirez nodded. Then he laid back and folded his hands behind his head, and stared up at the canvas. Wilson's footsteps receded into the distance.

He tried to imagine what his family would be doing right now. Back home it was probably 9pm, so Tracey would be putting Anna to bed. Anna was still at the age where she enjoyed a good bedtime story. Tracey would be laying on the bed next to Anna while she read one of those new chapter books out loud. Something fantastical, with faeries and elves and talking trees. Anna, laying her head on her mom's shoulder. Mom and daughter with the same beautiful curly, dark-brown hair.

Anna might last a chapter or two, and then her mom would climb out and go back to the couch to read her own book. Something… not nonfiction—

—historical fiction. That was it. Made-up stories, but grounded in reality (and probably romantic). The last one was about two lovers meeting on the Oregon Trail. Tracey had teared up just telling him about it.

Tracey would fall asleep on the couch with the book on her chest. Looking gorgeous and peaceful, like one of those pretty depictions of an angel.

No, that wasn't right either. California was behind. It was morning back home. Maybe Wilson was right. Maybe he should call Tracey.

It wasn't that Ramirez didn't want to call his wife. Quite the opposite. The two of them had never been the couple that talked on the phone every day of his deployments. Now there was so little he could tell her that… it was just *easier* when they didn't try to talk every day. He didn't have to skirt the details of his missions or about the things he saw, and it gave Tracey and Anna a sense of normalcy. Hopefully…

But Ramirez doubted his gut and as he lay there he realized that Wilson might be right; Atticus got those feelings about the missions sometimes and, dammit, the Sergeant was usually right. This mission *might* be different and Ramirez *should* call his wife again.

The soldier pulled out his sat-phone and called his wife. The phone rang and rang, and finally went to voicemail. Ramirez sighed. It could have been anything: Tracey left her phone on the couch while she was putting Anna to sleep or while she was in the kitchen cleaning up. He smiled as he thought about how she would leave the dishes until the end of the night and then insist on washing them before bed.

A few minutes later, Tracey called back.

"Hey baby," she said, surprise in her voice.

"Did I catch you in the middle of dishes again?"

"Every time. I dropped Anna off at school and just finished up the dishes from last night! We had tuna casserole for dinner. The Joneses stopped by and brought their girl, Charlie. Her and Anna have been doing homework together almost every day."

"I remember," Ramirez said with a smile. "It's about time she made another friend. How's your book?"

"Oh, well it's a rough one now."

"Like it wasn't rough when they crossed the river and lost a quarter of their supplies!"

Tracey chuckled at that. "Well, now they're passing through the mountains on the Oregon Trail and Charlotte's husband is suffering from a gangrene infection."

"Yep. They're going to amputate the bottom of his leg."

"That's why I'm glad I'm alive now and not two hundred years ago."

They shared a laugh and for a moment it was like Ramirez was back home, laying across the couch with his head in her lap while they talked. But soon their laughs faded and silence settled into the spaces inbetween, reminding him that he was on the other side of the world.

"We're going dark tomorrow, Trace," he said.

"Well, you said yesterday that it would be soon. I was surprised you called again—happy, just surprised."

Ramirez wasn't sure what to say. He didn't want to say that Atticus was worried because he didn't want his wife to worry.

"Just wanted to hear your voice again," he said. Hector imagined she was smiling but as the moment drug on worry seeped in with the silence. He turned to his usual sign off, "Tell Anna that I love her and to give Teddy a hug for me."

"I will."

"I'll call as soon as I can. Love you, Trace."

"Love you too."

They always left off on that note. It made it easier than accepting the fact that any mission could be his last. Omega Squad didn't exactly have a great survival rate, but then no one has a one-hundred percent guarantee.

Silence returned, but this silence wasn't oppressive or worrisome like it was when Tracey was on the line. This time it was familiar—comforting, even.

Ramirez laid on the bunk and shut his eyes. It was still too early to sleep, but his eyes were heavy. A few minutes later, he heard Wilson's voice.

"So did you call her?"

"Yeah, yeah," Ramirez replied without looking. "Happy now?"

"That my buddy is looking after his marriage? Sure. But then if you were single I wouldn't have to beg Tracey to let you go out to the bars."

Ramirez slapped blindly at the air to the side of the bunk and felt Wilson block it. Then the bed below him creaked as Wilson laid down on it. The two spent the rest of the short evening on their phones scrolling through nothing in particular. As the evening wore on, more and more soldiers turned in for the night.

In spite of the shit the two had seen in their tours with Omega and in spite of the bad vibes they were getting from the current mission, Ramirez slept as peacefully as the dead that night.

Omega Squad woke at 0400, had chow at 0410, introduced themselves to the translators at 0420, and at 0430 they followed Captain Miller through several more tents to an armory. Of all the makeshift buildings in outposts like these, the armory had several floor-to-ceiling steel cages inside to keep weapons and munitions secure. They always made Ramirez think of a pirate ship with holding cells.

The Sergeant in charge of the armory had set aside crates for them, all packed with weapons customized for the squad's current mission. Both Captain Miller and the Sergeant of the armory removed themselves and left the men to their preparations.

Lieutenant Ramirez ordered several of his soldiers to open the wooden shipping crates with pry bars and hammers. They made short work of the crates and a few seconds later his biblical suspicions from the previous night were confirmed.

Their M4 rifles and magazines were stamped with crosses. No one said a word, though the soldiers he knew to be Catholic signed a cross.

Lieutenant Ramirez bowed his head and the other Omega soldiers did the same. He led them through their creed:

"I am an Omega Soldier. I will bravely go to places that don't exist and against beings that strike fear into the hearts of men. I am a beacon in the darkness and a bastion against the occult. My will is incorruptible and my body is my own. *Mi voluntad es incorruptible y mi cuerpo es mío.*"

All soldiers repeated the last line of the creed in their native tongue as a ward. Using their mother tongue made the ward more powerful. It was one of the reasons Ramirez still prayed to himself in Spanish long after his grandfather passed.

Omega was made of soldiers from various religions (from careful curating) and so each soldier ended the creed in their own way: Several with "amen", others with "svāhā", or "namaste". Clark ended without saying anything at all—their token atheist.

Then each soldier reached for a weapon. An M4, as many rounds as they could carry, grenades laced with holy water and shrapnel from shaved crosses, silvered knives, and pouches filled with herbs and chalks.

When they were fully decked out in biblical perversions of modern-day weapons, Lieutenant Ramirez and Sergeant Wilson led the squad to the final muster area just outside the cave. The translators would be waiting.

~ ~ ~

Descent

Dr. David Levy

The alarm buzzed on David's wristwatch, jolting him out of the pitiful sleep he'd managed to get. The bright face of the watch didn't help and he had to squint to silence it. David couldn't remember the last time he'd woken up at 4:00 a.m.. Whenever it was, it certainly wasn't by choice.

Nancy groaned from the bunk just above him. Throughout the barracks a dozen other figures stirred in the dim light—the Omega Squad soldiers. They were up, dressed and out to the mess hall before Nancy had climbed down, even before David had found his pants.

The two translators dressed and stumbled half-asleep to the mess hall.

It made David feel better that Nancy was having a tough time waking up at that ungodly hour as well. He briefly thought about being the only man in the barracks having a tough time waking up, it was a fault of machismo that he rarely allowed himself; some urge to be stronger than Nancy purely because she was a woman. Which was absurd—they were both having trouble waking up because they were both *civilians* and not accustomed to it. It was not nothing to do with their biology.

Dammit, man. I'm an academic, not a soldier, David thought to himself in that familiar voice.

"What's so funny?" Nancy asked.

David waved it off. "The absurdity of the hour."

The cafeteria—mess hall—might have been the most decorated area of the base and seemed even more impressive this second time after having seen the rest of the base. It wasn't how David would've imagined the most constructed area of the base, but it made sense. Computers may have needed some wires, but cooking needed power and metal that simply couldn't be done wirelessly or made very compact.

The mess hall was even bigger than the barracks, but not quite as big as the main tent. The back of the room was taken up by a hulking, steaming monstrosity of a kitchen, which David imagined was either airlifted in by a humongous helicopter or (more likely) pieced together from several small deliveries.

In the middle of the room was a long buffet line. On the other side were rows and rows of all-in-one tables and chairs, like a grade school cafeteria. Sitting in the far corner was Omega Squad. They looked like they were already done eating.

Again, Nancy gave them a sheepish wave as they passed. The translators got served and then took a seat at an adjacent table. David and Nancy ate quietly. The special forces soldiers didn't offer any conversation, not even amongst themselves. David wondered if this much quiet was normal for the squad—it certainly wasn't normal for a mess hall, even at this ungodly hour. David wasn't sure what he expected, but the seriousness of the soldiers wasn't reassuring.

The mess was serving eggs with the consistency of jello. David mixed his hashbrowns with them and ate without thinking too much.

"It's not so bad," Nancy said, smiling in between bites.

"Eat up," said one of the special forces soldiers, a dark-skinned Latin man. He had a look of muted intensity about him. "You'll need the energy. It's about two miles through the caves to the first Staging Area. Half of it will be spelunking."

David recognized the single bar on his shirt collar, meaning that he was the commanding officer and likely in charge of the squad.

Both David and Nancy muttered, "Yes, sir," more in shock of actually talking to the squad than from the CO's demeanor. He turned back to his squad.

David had been about to ask a question when Nancy beat him to it. "Sir, could you tell us—"

"Ma'am, I'm not at liberty to discuss anything more than you've already been briefed." The CO's voice was calm and firm.

Nancy frowned at that.

A thin White soldier, with more stripes than the rest, added, "They haven't told us shit either." Some of the squad chuckled at the remark.

The CO added, "Standard Operating Procedure."

For the first time the squad and the translators shared a laugh, and then Captain Miller arrived to take the squad to the armory.

Two of them, the two that talked, stayed behind a moment with the translators and introduced themselves: Lieutenant Ramirez and Sergeant Wilson—the two in charge of the mission.

"Should we be going with you to the armory?" David asked.

The two soldiers shared a familiar smile. "Someone will come get you," the Lieutenant said. "They'll give you a vest and nonlethal protection."

Around 4:30 a.m. a base soldier led the translators through the canvassed hallways to a small room. Inside, several soldiers had laid out fatigues, helmets, body armor and an assortment of crosses and pendants.

David and Nancy were faced away from each other and instructed to stay still while they were measured for equipment. David found himself feeling self-conscious of his body, which was suffering from an astute case of academia. He mentally kicked himself for yet again having such a worry; he couldn't remember being this self-conscious the last time he worked with the army.

Thankfully, the measuring was over as quickly as it began. He put on the fatigues (just as scratchy as he remembered) and then was handed boots, and a kevlar vest and helmet. On the back of the vest were woven several geometric designs— runes—and another large cross. The helmet had similar designs woven into the cushion inside.

From behind him, Nancy asked, "Can you tell us about these symbols?"

One of the women soldiers replied, "No ma'am. These aren't standard equipment so I can't speak to them."

The kevlar was surprisingly thin and light, something familiar from the other mission. However, he also knew from that past mission that he would feel the extra weight after a mile or so. The helmet felt much the same and by the time everything was buckled, strapped and tightened, it felt like a second skin. A small flashlight was affixed to the side of the helmet.

When David finally turned and saw Nancy, she was smiling wide, clearly enjoying the novelty.

Then they were handed a collection of crosses and other holy symbols. David recognized some of them, namely Christian, Hebrew, Islamic, and Buddhist. Others Nancy identified as Hindi, Toaist, and even Wiccan. Lastly, they were given a multitool and two other small flashlights.

David had expected a weapon of some kind. He tried to hide his expression as he looked at the multitool.

The soldier said plainly, "Trust the squad. If it gets to the point where you need a weapon, then you won't need one for long."

Nancy missed the comment. Now David was starting to worry about what they'd signed up for. It was too much to process. Clearly something supernatural: Between the spirits and now the crosses and geometric symbols woven into their gear. And it was definitely dangerous, that much he felt in his gut.

Afterward one of the soldiers led them back to their alcove where their books and materials were so that they could gather the rest of the things they needed. Both Dr. Levy and Dr. Reed brought several small, leather-bound notebooks. One for each of Hebrew, Greek, Latin. Nancy brought another for Aramaic. They each grabbed extra pencils.

"I guess that's it then," she said. "Famous last words."

They shared an uneasy laugh and followed the soldier again, this time toward the cavern.

On the way they came across Omega Squad, now laden with helmets, weapons and arms.

They followed Omega soldiers down a long, straight hallway, passing two checkpoints along the way about thirty yards apart. Both were manned with a half a dozen soldiers. All of them were looking down the hallway, keeping watch.

Keeping watch on the dark crack in the rock at the opposite end—the cave entrance. The face of it was mottled grey and black, and, he supposed, normal enough for a cave. A cave that wasn't surrounded by a secret military outpost.

But as they got closer, a sense of quiet dread welled up inside of David. His stomach churned and his forehead grew damp from sweat. David could see that the tent butted up to the foot of a cliff. The rock face disappeared up above the opening of the tent and so he couldn't tell if the rock face went up thirty feet or up a mile. He quickly revoked his prior judgment about it being *normal enough*—It was ominous.

By the time they had finished the long hallway and entered the actual muster tent, he was in awe. The muster tent opened up, large enough to house a platoon—forty to fifty soldiers. Inside the two-story tent, two-dozen soldiers faced the entrance to the cave.

The entrance itself was about ten feet high, not quite as tall as the tent. A quiet breeze came from the cave; it was cool and smelled like rotten eggs.

Both David and Nancy covered their mouths. He had almost forgotten his colleague was next to him until she retched. Thankfully nothing came up.

"What's that smell?" she asked with a pinched nose.

One of the nearby soldiers answered, "It's the sulphur. You'll get used to it after a few minutes." Whoever answered hadn't looked away from the cave entrance. All eyes and all weapons were trained on the entrance. None of the special forces soldiers so much as coughed at the smell.

Then a hooded figure poked through the crevice, which seemed to startle no one except for the translators.

"Your guide is present." The man pulled back the hood to reveal a slender face, pronounced nose and brow, and dark-curled hair. He either wasn't wearing a vest or it was hidden beneath his robe. "Virgil, at your service. Are we ready to depart?"

Virgil had a heavy accent that was hard to place. It almost sounded Italian, but wasn't quite right. Either way, they must have found a diverse amount of languages to need both David and Nancy in addition to local help.

Just as soon as David's mind began to wander the group got ready to move out.

Lieutenant Ramirez stood at the mouth of the cavern beside Virgil. He turned to address them. "From here out there is no going back. Keep communication to the necessities. We will reassess once we get to the First Staging area."

And with that small ceremony Omega Squad turned on flashlights and went single-file into the cave. Dr. Levy and Dr. Reed were ushered into the middle of the procession.

The cave was narrow, so much so that they were always single file and often had to shimmy sideways through gaps. The walls were cool and damp with occasional streams falling through from some unseen water source above and down into some undisclosed crevices beneath their feet. The thought of slipping on the slick rocks crossed David's mind, but thankfully there were no wide crevices in which to fall and disappear.

It was a thought he didn't dwell on long because the team moved in a steady procession.

"Eventually the cavern will widen," Virgil said, his voice echoing through the narrow passages. "Do not despair."

For most of the procession, the steady shuffling of feet, and keeping pace with the soldier in front and behind him was all that David could focus on. Step, step, shuffle, shuffle. It was taxing in its own way, but he much preferred this mild spelunking to a march over flat ground, where his mind had nothing else to focus on but the slowly-building soreness in his legs and lungs.

Even if he had the nerve to converse, two soldiers were in line between David and Nancy, presumably to help them if either needed it.

David dared not look at the time, but he guessed that an hour had passed from the start of their journey until the cave finally, mercifully opened up.

"My God," David muttered.

There was misty light at the end of the cavern and one-by-one he watched the soldiers disappear into the opening as they fanned around the corners.

The soldier directly in front of him turned and took David's arm to guide him around the corner and ushered him to duck while Omega Squad confirmed their safety.

The cavern had opened—blossomed—around them. The ceiling rose up at least a hundred feet, its full height blocked by the bright mist that filled the area. The cavern disappeared off to either side in the same fashion—covered by mist. Around them, green and orange moss stretched over the floor, so thick it looked like grass. Several massive structures rose up into the mist, nearly the color of gray stone; David finally realized that they were trees.

The mist above them flashed white and a thunderclap stuttered, eerie and beautiful.

Nancy and her accompanying soldier crouched on the opposite side of the cave opening. She looked around with the same jaw-dropped look. The rest of the soldiers, however, looked around with weapons, searching both the ground and the mist-covered air above them.

Virgil turned to address the group, unimpressed by the sight and unperturbed by the soldiers' vigilance. "You will see and hear a great many things as you pass through this cavern. It is deep and its wonders are many. Do not engage with anything you perceive. The vast majority of what you will experience in this part of the cavern is not dangerous in the slightest."

David caught Nancy's eye from the other side of the entrance. She heard it too. *This part* of the cave wasn't dangerous. Before his mind could wander, the soldier with him gently pulled David to his feet.

The squad crept out into the mist. The translators walked timidly in the center of the group along with Virgil, who seemed perfectly at ease. The soldiers encircled them in a diamond formation. They walked in a half crouch, rifles shouldered and ready. A dozen rifle barrels always faced outward—in spite of what their guide said—ready for any dangers that might lurk out there.

David found himself entranced by the coordination, but only half able to pay attention. He couldn't take his eyes off the fog. Nancy was also looking around quickly. It was as if they could *feel* something watching them, feel something out there.

Then they heard it: Human voices all around them. Muttering unintelligibly. Everyone slowed and finally stopped. Feverish eyes scanned the veil of fog.

Virgil was the only one that seemed unperturbed. "We shouldn't dawdle," he said. "Not until we reach the First Staging Area. There is nothing to fear from the poor bastards out there or those above us."

Virgil looked up and all eyes followed his gaze. From somewhere in the mist-covered cavern a gigantic, feathered wingtip descended. The feathers were speckled white and brown and grazed a tree next to them. The wing was many times thicker than the tree and it shuddered from the glancing blow.

"Get down!" one of the soldiers roared and the squad knelt down, making themselves small against the colossal scene. David dropped to the ground and put his arms over his head and neck. He watched the scene through squinted eyes.

As quickly as the wing descended it was gone and in its wake, three more wings fell and rose in procession as if they were a part of the same titanic creature. The poor tree shuddered with each blow, but the ground didn't rumble.

It was only as the last wing rose out of sight that David realized no wind had blown in their procession. The moss hadn't so much as moved from the wings. In the mist above, thunder rumbled and followed the trail of the creature.

"What was that?" the lanky Sergeant whispered.

"Nothing to fear," Virgil replied, calmly. "But we mustn't dawdle."

From somewhere in the mist around them, the mutterings began again. Much, much closer than the distant thunder.

It didn't take long to find the source of the muttering. A figure lay sprawled out on the ground, whispering. They walked closer still and saw it was a ragged old woman in white robes, filthy with dirt and grass stains. She was breathing steadily and though she was contorted on the ground, she didn't look distressed. She didn't so much as glance their direction.

David felt a pain in his chest, a desire to help her, even though he didn't know what she needed.

"Sir?" one of the soldiers up front asked, concern in his voice. David imagined the same thought ran through his mind too.

"Do not touch her," Virgil said. He looked at the woman with disdain, his voice nearly a sneer. "There is nothing you could do for her and nothing she would want you to do for her. She is little different from the impotent creatures that fly above us."

Out in the mist came more groans.

Virgil continued, "There are uncountable many like her, powerless, fated to continue on as they did in life."

Nearly every head snapped toward Virgil. The soldiers all went back to their surveillance of the fog, but David and Nancy stared at their stoic guide.

In a shaking voice, David asked, "What do you mean? Is she dead?"

Virgil chuckled. "Oh no, good scholar. These poor unre-solved souls cannot even reside themselves to death. That is why they're here: Men and women who could not choose or took advantage with no minds of their own. Angels who could not choose between their maker and their brother.

"The true tragedy," Virgil added with a wave of his finger, "is that they could leave at any time, if they would only choose."

Some of the soldiers exchanged glances but none of them wanted to look at their guide. How could Virgil be so callous? What was he even talking about? David looked to Nancy, but she was frozen as well, staring at Virgil. The woman—what-ever thing—she was, mumbled steadily on the ground.

Questions went through David's head as he glanced be-tween the squad, his guide, and his fellow translator. Would no one ask? Would no one ask where they were? Where were they going?

"We shouldn't dawdle."

"Move out," the Commander said.

Again they walked deeper into the fog, following Virgil's gestures. They passed more poor people laying on the ground. Men, women, some in robes, some in business suits, some in tribal dress.

Two reached out with a feeble hand toward the group, barely lifting an arm off the ground. The squad walked around them easily.

"Hold," the Commander said.

Before David could wonder why they had stopped, he heard the mutterings in earnest. "*Arbitrium derelinquam.*" *...Fore-saken choice.* "*No spem nobis.*" *...We have no hope.*

Then David looked ahead. To why the group stopped. In front of them was a man in rags, standing in front of them. His clothes were tattered and his face was completely blank: There was skin over his eyes sockets, his nose was flat and formless. His mouth was gone… He had no lips or even an opening.

The man just stood there while weapons were leveled at him. Finally the Squad walked around him, but not before the man raised a thin boned hand toward the Lieutenant, which followed the soldier as they walked around.

They left him behind in the mist; he didn't walk or turn to follow them.

They walked by a dozen more people. Most lay still on the ground, muttering incoherently. Only two more stood upright. Again the figures gestured toward the Lieutenant but didn't turn to follow them.

David breathed a sigh of relief when the mist gave way to another cavern wall and at the center, another cracked opening like the one they passed through at the beginning. The translator would've much rather been claustrophobic than back with whatever those *things* were.

"We must go through," Virgil commanded. David wondered how many times Virgil had made the journey to be as stoic as he was.

Once more Omega squad and the translators inched their way through narrow caverns, but this time David was glad to be back in the confines and away from the creatures that hid in the mist. He nearly laughed to himself that the dark passageway was more comforting.

~

Lieutenant Hector Ramirez

Again the cavern gave way to an opening. Omega Squad gathered just outside of the opening to take stock of their situation before moving further.

This time the cavern was relatively clear. Mist only floated and obscured the furthest reaches of their sight. The cavern was low and wide, easily several hundred yards across, and partially lit by the river that stretched across it. The air still had the faintest whiff of sulphur.

When the Lieutenant was satisfied that the cavern was clear, he waved for a soldier to check the river.

"It is a dangerous thing," Virgil said. He looked at the river with awe. "Do not touch its waters."

The soldier nodded and approached within a few feet. The green waters glowed and reflected on his fatigues.

"Clear."

Lieutenant Ramirez signaled for the squad to move closer and they stopped again on the shore of the river.

From there, they could see that the river was roughly thirty yards across. The water was smooth and green, and moving slowly. Its rocky shore dropped to shallows and then into a crevice that dropped down out of sight. Inside the crevice was an impossibly bright green.

If it were anything like the other supernatural things that Ramirez had seen during his time with Omega, the river dropped into an infinite abyss. One that wrenched the soul from the body and did all other manner of horrible shit to a person.

Across the water was another shore and another cave. Their robed guide confirmed that that was their destination.

"How are we going to cross that?" Sergeant Wilson asked. "You said we can't get in the water."

Virgil nodded. "A mortal cannot cross the river Acheron, nor can they swim in its waters. It would drag you under and smash your body against the rocks."

"That would be a fun way to die," Wilson replied sarcastically.

"Oh, one would not die for a very long time. You would be in a stasis of drowning and agony until your body rotted and dissolved and finally became indistinguishable from the waters. Then your soul would dissolve into nothingness sometimes later, giving the water its beautiful glow."

An awkward moment passed before Lieutenant Ramirez spoke up. "How are we supposed to cross the river?"

Virgil looked idly off across the green river—upriver. "We wait. The boatman will take us across."

The translators glanced nervously around but Omega squad paid them no mind. Ramirez was used to cryptic answers like these. Supernatural answers for supernatural problems.

"How long?" The Lieutenant asked.

"He comes now."

All eyes were watching upriver. Slowly, a ship rounded the cave wall. It was broad and flat, nearly half the width of the river. Above water it was little more than a floating platform. It glided across the river Acheron like a Venice gondola.

As the massive gondola rounded the bend of the river, a towering figure came into view. From afar it was little more than a robed figure, its head nearly brushing the top of the cavern. The cavern was shorter than previous sections, but it was still fifteen feet high in the shortest areas—the boatman was easily thirteen feet tall.

And as it came closer, its features came into view: Twisted skeleton hands gripped the pushing pole which moved with methodical certainty. Ramirez had seen the same proficiency in sailors that had spent their lives and livelihoods on perilous waters. But the boatman was inhumanly steady as if the creature had rowed Acheron far longer than any fisherman had lived.

The barge thumped to a stop against the rocks of the shore. The boatman waited. The translators in the center of the group were breathing shallow and quick.

Up close, they saw the boatman clearly. His robe was massive and made of thick fiber. His face and feet were the same nearly-bare skeleton as his hands. There were no muscles or skin covering him, but tendons and ligaments stretched and pulsed as the giant moved, bulging beneath the cloak as if creatures were living under it.

His skull had a crisscrossing of tendons which Ramirez could only assume was normal of a human skull, but the boatman had no eyes. It's sockets were deep black pits, so deep that the back of the skull wasn't visible. The creature didn't look away from the river or acknowledge them in the slightest.

Virgil was the first to step from the rocks and onto the barge. The green waters almost seemed to recede from the rocks as he did. Before anyone could protest, the guide said, "Come. Do not fear Charon. One thing you should learn here is that the things that appear the most frightening are often the least so… and innocuous, beautiful or familiar things are often damning."

Before anyone could argue with Virgil's cryptic message, Ramirez ordered Omega Squad onto the barge.

Predictably, Dr. Levy asked, "Where exactly is *here*?"

Virgil grinned deviously as Charon pushed away from the shore. In spite of their numbers and the herculean task of moving the barge, the creature pushed them away so smoothly that no one, not even the translators, shifted on their feet.

Though no weapons were pointed at Charon, damn near every soldier kept the creature in the corner of their vision.

It was only after they were away from the shore, with no hope of return that Virgil answered the question.

"There are many names for where we're going, none of which you will believe. We will be at the first staging area soon, just beyond the doorway. There you will learn the truth, for you would not believe me if I told you."

Inexorably, the barge moved across the river Acheron. The creaks of the pushing pole and the snaps of the boatman's tendons were the only sounds.

Once on the other side, Ramirez gave the order to disembark and his squad was quick to oblige. Behind them, Virgil dropped coins into the giant, gnarled hand of the boatman—the significance of the gesture that was not lost on him.

The lieutenant looked over his squad and read their faces. They searched the cavern for signs of danger with tactical—mechanical—efficiency and yet he knew they felt uneasy. He knew this because he felt uneasy.

A dozen missions into places as strange as this, or stranger even. The mimetic virus that jumped from mind to mind or the skinwalkers of the Amazon. Then there was bezymyannoye mesto—*the nameless place* in the frozen bowels of Russia; that one might be the closest. It wasn't any one thing giving him signals… It was that the entire place felt wrong.

Again Omega Squad and the translators shuffled through narrow caverns. This was already some of the most spelunking that Ramirez and his squad had ever done on a mission and it showed no signs of ending.

The caves weren't so bad, Ramirez decided, not compared to the mist. Even the boatman didn't creep him out as much as those things in the mist had. The worst part about the caves was that it gave him time to dwell on things like that.

While they were in the mist he had the eerie feeling that the creatures had been reaching out to him instead of at the squad. Even the mist itself had felt ominous. Maybe in another life it would have been him slack jawed on the floor of the cavern, pawing at whatever poor bastards wandered through the mist.

A few seconds later the caverns opened up again, sparing him from dwelling on the thought. Ramirez and the squad filed into the small cavern and came face-to-face with the doorway.

~

Dr. David Levy

The alcove was the size of a small room. Just enough room for the team to stand shoulder-to-shoulder inside it. Packing bodies into the alcove made David even more claustrophobic than the thin caverns they passed through. He felt the hot stale air from the dozen people filling the room—it seemed as if everyone but him was breathing steadily. Mercifully the ceiling rose up at least twelve feet; David found himself tilting his head back to get fresher air. Nancy and two other soldiers in front of him had similar ideas.

It was in that alcove they found the doorway.

At first he could only see the top stones of the arch above the helmets of the soldiers in front of him. Then the soldiers had shuffled and turned to allow him and Nancy to walk forward. All eyes and helmet-mounted flashlights were on the doorway.

The doorway was made of stacked stones that rose up to an arched top as high as the ceiling of the cavern. In his travels, David had seen plenty of architecture and none of it had made his skin crawl like these doors did.

The stones were not perfectly square but they were stacked in such a way that the two sides of the doorway were even and parallel, and so the doorway fit neatly inside the stone of the cavern. There were no gaps or even mortar or smaller stones were present around the sides. The doors were also made of stone, fit and sealed perfectly to the stone arch.

David decided that was the eerie reason—it was perfectly symmetrical. Inhuman. At the very least, it was out of place in the natural cracks and openings of the cavern.

While David stood speechless from the architecture of the doorway, Nancy had stooped forward to read the writing that covered the doorway.

She slapped his leg. "Look at this."

It was enough to snap David out of his trance. He leaned over and looked closer.

Writing covered every inch of the stone doorway, but it quickly became clear that it wasn't written in any one language. No two languages seemed the same. David recognized some of the romance languages, though he couldn't read them, but there were others, Russian or possibly Ukranian, Sanskrit-like languages, and even those resembling Asian scripts.

The Lieutenant muttered something in Spanish.

Dr. Reed pointed toward the doors themselves. There were the ancient languages David recognized. The same phrase was written in Hebrew, Greek and Latin:

התקווה את נטוש הנה נכנס אשר אתה.
Εγκαταλείψτε όλους ελπίζουμε να μπείτε εδώ.
Qui deserit sperantes ingredieris huc.

David looked at the other dozens—hundreds maybe—of languages written across the stones. His heart pounded. He felt like he was swimming in sweat, suffocating in the recycled air of the soldiers sandwiched around him.

He imagined every written language of man chiseled into those stones—A warning that no one could possibly miss.

Then he saw the words in English:

Abandon all hope you who enter here.

His chest tightened. Fingers numb.

"David. David!" Nancy grabbed his arms and shook him but she was far away. The soldiers were gone. The cave was a distant memory. He was standing in blackness, alone with the doorway.

The doorway seemed to grow, rising up and finally towering over him like the trees in the mist-covered cave. The words glowed and whispered to him in all the languages of human-kind—whispering all around him. He felt the cold breath of the dead on his ears and across his bare neck. They seeped under his helmet and shirt, like ice water seeping through his clothes.

"David!" Nancy's voice, closer.

The darkness receded. The walls of the cave came back into view. The cold breath of death replaced with the muggy breath of a dozen soldiers, armed with weapons for whatever super-natural dangers awaited them.

Nancy shook him again. "Hold it together, David." She smiled, but it was nervous, one that seemed to barely contain her own fear.

The soldiers of Omega Squad made a point of looking down or at the doorway. David was thankful for that bit of dignity.

"I'm here," he said quietly. "I'm here."

Now the Lieutenant leaned in toward the translators. His voice was firm and sure, as if he was trying to steady Dr. Levy with it alone.

"We're not here for the doorway."

With that, Virgil shuffled forward and pushed on the two stone doors. They gave way, swinging open with eerie silence;

there was no sound of any gears or clicking of locks or whisper of stone hinges.

Beyond the doorway was a passageway, wide enough for them to walk through. One-by-one the soldiers walked through the doorway, paying the warnings no mind. Even Nancy went through.

David was pushed through the doorway by the soldiers behind him. He felt swept up in a current and for a moment he imagined that he had slipped into the waters of Acheron—that he was powerless and moments away from being smashed on the rocks.

~ ~ ~

Staging Area Alpha

Lieutenant Hector Ramirez

Omega Squad walked deeper into the cavern, into the unknown. Ramirez kept his eyes on the translators. Of the two, Dr. Levy seemed the worse, but he knew that could change in an instant. Everyone had their triggers: For some it was spiders, for others it was humanoid creatures, for others it was the unknown itself.

Just as quickly as Dr. Levy lost his composure, Dr. Reed could do the same. No one was immune to that fear.

His squad had training to protect their bodies, and—more importantly—to protect their minds. On top of that, they had seen horrors before, supernatural and unexplained ones; that kind of experience was as important as the training. Even with all that, no one in the squad would pretend they were immune to that fear. They all felt it, but now they could push past it or operate in spite of it.

Ramirez pitied the poor translators. They didn't have the same training. Likely didn't believe in the supernatural. This kind of mission could be a hell of a shock. Yet Ops kept send-ing them fresh civilians when needed.

He just hoped Dr. Levy and Dr. Reed could hold it together long enough to do what needed to be done—whatever that was. They wouldn't know until they made it to the Staging Ar-eas.

The cavern opened up. Rock walls gave way to grass and trees and mist. Ramirez thought that somehow they had gotten turned around, but this cavern was different. There were no whispers and no crackling of thunder above—nothing to sug-gest that dangers lurked just inside the mist. The mist wasn't oppressive and blinding like it had been in the cave before the river, Acheron. Here it was softly lit and they could see for one hundred yards in either direction.

Houses and tents were in the distance. People and soldiers.

The first Staging Area.

"Friendlies!" Ramirez announced as they approached.

The soldiers in the distance stood in a trench, their heads and shoulders peeking out above it. Only one of the three was watching the cavern entrance. He waved half-heartedly.

Several of them breathed a sigh of relief as they approached. The mist gave way to a town.

Ramirez led them to the Army soldiers at the head of the town. One of them, a muddy corporal, walked up the slope and saluted. Ramirez set him at ease.

"Omega Squad, reporting."

"Sir, you'll want to see Major Cobb. He's in town."

Ramirez eyed the private. He thought briefly about correct-ing the lazy scene he came upon, but relaxed. Ten years ago he would have, but not now. Not for these poor regulars who had crossed the mist and the barge and whatever else. So Ramirez nodded and waved Omega Squad into the town.

There were rows and streets filled with single homes. Each made of wood and mud walls with a thatched roof. Ramirez remembered walking through a historic town with his mother and seeing similar buildings. It was a technique from the 1600 or 1700's—possibly even older.

Plainly said, it wasn't the type of house the Army would commission.

The streets around them were dirt and sparse grass, worn from foot traffic and presumably wagon traffic, though Ramirez didn't see any horses or wagons.

The people that walked the streets had the same look of being lifted out of history. A portion were dressed in the plain clothes of settlers. Others wore long robes like their guide, Virgil. Others wore clothes made of animal pelts; some of which could've been Native American but others looked decidedly European or maybe Norse.

Ramirez glanced around, trying to process what he was seeing. It seemed as if people from all periods of history had been dropped into this town. There were people in tribal dress from the oldest civilizations all the way through to dozens of people in jeans and T-shirts.

And on marked corners were U.S. Army soldiers, looking just as lax as the post at the entrance to the city.

A group of children ran past, some in overalls and others in tunics. They chased each other and laughed as they looped around the soldiers and then ran off between the thatched houses.

At what appeared to be the center, several two-story buildings dominated a circle. These were made of brick and shingles. Dozens of men and women in all manner of dress talked and wandered. There was even a group of Greecian soldiers talking with Army regulars.

A group of soldiers pointed Omega toward the governor's office, where Major Cobb was staying. Ramirez ordered Omega to stay outside while he talked to Major Cobb.

The Lieutenant knocked and entered without waiting for an answer. Inside, the governor's office was ornate with shiny floorboards and hand-carved fixtures. Lace covered everything. Ramirez pictured the frills of an English nobleman's suit splayed all over the room like a trapper might have decorated with furs.

Down a short hallway and past several offices was a large open ballroom with a dozen men conversing in three small groups. Some wore long deep-colored robes, like Virgil wore, while others wore the dress of the frills of an Englishman. They should've left them on the furniture with the rest.

Ramirez's boots echoed on the floorboards but no one so much as looked in his direction. He stopped at the edge of the ballroom. There he saw the lanky major talking freely.

"Major Cobb," Ramirez said over the room. Several glanced his way, but the conversations continued without interruption.

Major Cobb excused himself and walked over. "What can I do for you… Lieutenant?" His shirt was buttoned loosely and three days' worth of stubble covered his face. Bags hung under his eyes.

"Omega Squad, reporting. We were told that we would receive briefings at each Staging Area."

The Major scoffed. "Is Colonel Jensen still in charge?" Ramirez nodded. "No wonder he didn't want to tell you." He led the Lieutenant back down the hallway to one of the offices.

Cobb lit several fat candles around the room before the two officers sat in the stiff wooden chairs. Cobb pulled out two lowball glasses and a half-full bottle of brown liquor—label torn off.

"I don't drink on mission, sir," Ramirez interrupted.

Cobb shrugged. He set one glass to the side and poured himself a finger's worth. "Do you know where you are, Lieutenant?"

"We're in a pocket dimension. Powerful beings create a separate plane of existence where they can bend reality. Shape it. Create things—even people."

The senior officer smiled and swirled his drink, watching intently. "I was wondering what lingo your guys would put on it. I only heard you were coming a few days ago. I didn't even know there was a supernatural branch of Spec Ops."

"Most don't," Ramirez said, allowing himself to crack a smile.

"You've seen some shit though? That right?"

"More than most, sir."

"Not like this." Cobb drank to punctuate the remark.

Ramirez shook his head. "I'm sure this is rough for you, sir, but my men have seen supernatural beings, even combat, across the globe. That's why they brought us here. It's what we do."

The Major stared at him. His eyes were red and he was barely holding it together. Ramirez had seen it in hundreds of soldiers and civilians that had run up against the supernatural.

"They didn't tell you where you were going," he said. "If they told you, you wouldn't have come."

"Tell me then. Where do you think we are, sir? And don't be cryptic like our guide."

Cobb rolled his eyes. "Virgil… In another life he would've made a good CO. He won't tell you either. No one will come right out and say it, but I'll tell you." He finished the glass and sighed. "I've been holding out as much as I can," he gestured to the bottle. "My wife would be proud of me."

The two men stared at the bottle in silence like maybe it would offer up the answer. Ramirez knew for a fact that it wouldn't.

"You're in Hell," the CO said, keeping his eyes on the bottle.

The word chilled the air, like a swift breeze had passed through. Ramirez fought a shiver. Candlelight around the room flickered.

"No one will come out and say it, but that's where we are— on the outskirts of it. I think this is Limbo: It's where the pagan's—nonbelievers—who lived decent lives came."

"That's quite a claim, sir—"

"You go further in, you'll see what I mean." The Major stared at him, warning him. "It's divided into circles. Going deeper means passing through the circles." He paused to pour another drink. "There's a reason why the Staging Area Bravo doesn't push further in. They lost a lot of men already. It's safe in Alpha. The men here don't know. I intend to keep it that way."

Rather than concede the Major's point, Ramirez asked, "What should we look out for?"

"Keep an eye on your own men. It's not about what they *will* do. It's about what they've done. Do you understand?"

The Lieutenant shook his head.

"Do you still have all your men? Have any of the souls reached out to them yet?"

Just Ramirez, himself. His voice nearly caught in his throat. "Just some of the souls in the first section." When he couldn't remember how Virgil described that section, he added, "The lazy section."

The Major nodded. "That's what they do. They sense your failings. They know your sins. They reach out for other souls that belong with them. Command is having a bitch of a time reinforcing Staging Area Bravo.

"That's your mission: Get to Bravo. They'll tell you more."

"Have you gone ahead?"

Cobb shook his head. "I won't. I know exactly where they'd get me."

Ramirez eyed the old Major and briefly wondered if it was the bottle or if it was some other sin he was referring to.

Maybe, just maybe, he was right about this place. What then? They had their mission and Alpha wasn't it. They had to continue on.

Instead of staying to ask more, Lieutenant Ramirez stood and saluted the Major. The CO returned a salute without standing or so much as looking at him. Another soldier might've taken offence, but Ramirez knew—he knew the moral dilemma that churned in the Major. It was the lonely conflict of a man sending others off to die.

Ramirez knew because he felt that same hollowness, like his insides were gone and replaced with the churning of the low-ball glass. The Lieutenant paused at the door.

Major Cobb must have heard his footsteps stop. He called from the office, "What will you tell them?"

He would tell them the same thing he always did—what he was ordered to.

"What they need to hear."

~

Dr. David Levy

Dr. Levy and Dr. Reed waited outside of the governor's building with the rest of Omega Squad.

David desperately wanted to sit, and so he plopped down beside the building and reclined against it. There was a distant voice somewhere in his mind urging him not to sit, lest his legs cramp up from the long walk, but he didn't give a shit. He had seen too much and his mind needed as much of a break as his legs did.

Nancy sat down beside him, sitting criss-cross and leaning on her elbows. The soldiers all relaxed. Several laid down on their backs without taking their packs off, which caused their necks to rest at odd angles. David wasn't sure how any of that could've been comfortable, but then he supposed the soldiers were used to resting and sleeping in odd positions.

The two translators shared a half-smile and nothing more. The soldiers talked. David listened, hoping to gleam information about where they were, but they talked about anything but.

They talked about home: Some about wives waiting for them, three laughed about girlfriends *and* wives waiting for them. Others talked about gambling and cards at the casino. Another about beating up his wife's boyfriend.

Maybe it was a defense mechanism that didn't allow the soldiers to talk about where they were. Some way of keeping their minds occupied. To David, it felt odd. How could they think about anything else? Maybe they had just seen it all and this current mission was just like any other.

Well, it was certainly something to David and it looked like Nancy was having a rough time of it too.

It just didn't make sense... Virgil had talked about souls and mortals. Then there were those wings and the boatman! David shuddered at the thought of the gigantic skeleton boatman.

And what did Virgil mean when he said that things that looked frightening, weren't so, and that inconspicuous things would be frightening? David eyed their cryptic guide; he was off fraternizing with other natives. Just what was that cook talking about?

"Are you alright, David?"

Nancy's voice startled him, but he nodded. As well as can be expected, given the circumstance." He gestured to the supernatural town all around him. "How can they not talk about all this?"

Nancy eyed the soldiers. "Maybe they're right to keep their minds off of it? Let's talk about something else too. Just think of the papers we can write when we get back!" Again she smiled half-heartedly.

"I could finally get into Columbia with that."

"Or Princeton."

"You think?" he asked.

"Certainly. We'll co-author it. People would eat it up. We could turn it into seminars and be set for life."

"Wait, you're not actually considering it? Are you?" David asked.

Nancy shrugged. "Oh, the government might not let us, but oh, if they did! Could you imagine? There's no harm in asking.

We just have to keep our wits about us, just have to make it out of here.

David smiled. "They'll swear us to secrecy. It's standard fare for classified missions."

"You think?" She asked playfully. "Of course. Of course. You're right. A gal can dream though, can't she? I would never—I mean, we—would never have to publish another paper again."

It was a nice thought, one that David allowed himself. One that ended abruptly.

The Lieutenant stepped out of the governor's house and immediately the soldiers rolled off of their backs and to their feet. Dr. Levy and Dr. Reed did the same, though it took them a few seconds longer.

The CO sighed and looked around at every soldier and translator.

"Some of you want answers and explanations. Well, I don't have much. We're in a pocket dimension—a universe inside our own. This isn't the first time Omega Squad has encountered one and there's no reason to believe that it will be any different this time.

"The deeper we go, the higher our chances of encountering danger." The Lieutenant turned to David and Nancy and added, "That's what we're here for. We've fought supernatural beings on every continent and we've won every time.

"Now the command inside here doesn't know much, and most regulars don't, but he did have one piece of intel. This dimension is more psychologically dangerous than physically dangerous. The CO said to watch out for your vices and be weary of temptation. Whatever supernatural beings lurked here will use those vices and virtues against you. So be ready for them.

"Our mission is to get to the next point, Staging Area Bravo. Get some food and rest. Meet back here in two hours. Dismissed. "

With that, the Lieutenant walked off into town, leaving David and the others to contemplate the dangers they would face.

David and Nancy followed Omega Squad deeper into the old-time town. David felt numb. He had expected answers from the Lieutenant. Instead their CO had looked more disturbed than ever.

Clearly he had learned something in his meeting with Staging Area command. Something that he wasn't telling the rest of them. David whispered this to Nancy.

"I think you're being paranoid," she replied quickly, as if she was trying to convince herself rather than him. "Maybe it's better not to know."

David shook his head.

They stopped at a store-tent and got in line for rations, where soldiers passed out packaged lunches, Meals-Ready-to-Eat (MRE). Soldiers ate nearby at a picnic area with thin wooden furniture. David wondered briefly if the townsfolk had furnished the area for the soldiers, but the smell of food from nearby tables pushed it out of his mind.

Soldiers talked quietly around them, occasionally bursting into laughter. The two translators sat on the end of one of the empty tables. David's back was to the town. The grassy field receded off into the mist.

"We're all a little mad down here," Nancy said with a giggle as she tore open her MRE.

"Excuse me?"

"Alice in Wonderland. All we're missing is tea."

"Oh." David managed a smile. He set to the task of explaining how to mix the packaged water with the chemical heater to make a warm meal out of Nancy's meatballs and marinara. She loved the invention.

Then he made his own chicken burrito bowl, which thankfully tasted better than it looked.

"You don't look like the others," a little girl said from beside them.

David jumped and both the little girl and Nancy laughed.

"I'm sorry, mister," she added. When David caught his breath he turned and saw her, dressed like a little settler in a brown dress, hair bunned up. He chuckled at being startled by someone so small and precious. She reminded him of his niece.

"You'll have to forgive him," Nancy said to the girl.

"You're not soldiers are you? Why are you here?" the girl asked.

"We're translators," David replied. "We know how to read and write other languages."

Her face scrunched up in confusion. "Are their other languages in the town? I've never heard anything else or seen anything else written."

Nancy and David shared a look. Nancy asked, "What about the other peoples in your town? Haven't you heard languages you don't recognize?"

The girl shook her head. "No, even my friends that dress funny all speak the same language."

Virgil's voice came from the opposite side of the table. "Everyone speaks and hears their mother-tongue, no matter the dialect or time period." He walked around to Nancy's side as he talked and sat in the chair next to her. "There are no misunderstandings here. Run along child."

"Yes, sir. Virgil, sir."

David and Nancy watched her run back into town.

"She knew your name," Nancy remarked. "You must get around."

"It's my duty here. I am a guide to more than just American soldiers and translators."

"She might have told us more about this place," David said, turning around. He glared at Virgil. "Are you going to be honest with us and tell us what's going on?"

Virgil stared at him plainly, in spite of the anger that had to be on David's face. "I will consider it, so long as you do not disturb the dead."

As the last word was spoken, David's anger drained away and he felt hollow again. He had known when they saw the spirits in the woods and when he stood in front of the doorway.

They had passed into the realm of the dead.

"...Is this Heaven?" Nancy asked with the same look of disbelief.

Virgil scoffed and propped his elbows on the table. "Does this look like your idea of Heaven? This is a place for pagans, for skeptics and non-believers; the righteous and the faithless."

"Then it's purgatory?" Nancy asked.

Virgil waved dismissively. "You ask the wrong questions."

"We should've stuck with the kid," David said.

The guide continued, "Why do none of the townspeople eat or drink? Why do they never age? You might think those easy, for they are mortal things and the townspeople are dead.

"Why does everyone speak the same language here? That is harder, but easy once you understand *why* the people are here." When David and Nancy didn't answer, Virgil continued. "The people are here for what they lacked and in many terms these people lacked for nothing: They loved their neighbors, lived noble lives, helped their fellow man, pursued pure reason and truth. Here they are free to continue on as they did in life."

David looked off at the mist-covered town and thought that this surely couldn't be Heaven. But then it couldn't be Hell either. It seemed far too merciful a fate. Was this Purgatory? Why was he still thinking in Christian terms?

Virgil interrupted his thoughts. "Alas, I have already said too much about this place. The truth is something that you must realize for yourself."

David leaned back in his chair, silently cursing the cryptic guide.

Thankfully Nancy thought of something else. "So are we supposed to ask about you then? Why are you here?"

Virgil shrugged. "In life I was a story-teller, a poet. I thought that I could guide others to knowledge through my stories. Either I used my gifts too well, and was rewarded with a fitting afterlife, or I did my job poorly and was punished in much the same fashion."

"Why guide us down here then?" David asked. "Why let us down here?"

Virgil smiled at that. "Now there is a question, good scribe, and I am happy to tell you that particular answer: *Sometimes mortals need to see to believe.*"

Virgil left the translators alone at the table. Alone with their thoughts, amidst the soldiers and the dead that wandered the streets. The dead that carried on just as they had in life.

"So we're in Purgatory then," David said quietly. He said the words but he didn't *believe* them—not in a physical sense, or in a spiritual sense. David was an atheist... Was he trying to convince himself?

Nancy picked at the ridges in the picnic table. "Do you believe that?" She looked up at him with watery eyes.

His heart went out to her. David reached out a thin hand and she took it. Her skin was cool and clammy.

"No," David said. "I think that's what Virgil and the spirits want us to believe. This is a trick or a shared hallucination. There were thousands of religions... The soldiers even said that they've seen pocket dimensions and things like that."

"But this is the afterlife, David. The things we've seen, the spirits."

"I don't think this is Purgatory."

"You're not a Christian then?"

He shrugged. "I was raised Baptist. Went to church every Sunday. But the more I learned, I just fell out of it. This might be the afterlife, or maybe even *an* afterlife—if that's a thing. I just haven't found a religion that I felt *got it right.*"

"Maybe that's best," Nancy replied. Her voice quivered.

David scrunched his face in question, but before he could reply—

"I know where we are." But she would not give voice to the answer.

~ ~ ~

The Hallway

Lieutenant Hector Ramirez

Two hours passed restlessly for the Lieutenant. He slumped against one of the homes along the road and watched towns-folk pass by.

The Major thought this was Limbo; where good pagans went. Ramirez wasn't sure what to think—other than that everyone seemed dead by the usual standards. He tried to imagine each passing family somewhere in the real world in whatever time they came from: Settlers, pilgrims, tribesmen.

Tried to think about anything other than where they were, where they were going, and how spirits had reached out to him in the misty woods before the river Acheron. Virgil called them *unresolved souls*. Men and angels that hadn't chosen... chosen what? Why would they reach out to Ramirez? He believed. He had believed in the Lord all his life.

The Lieutenant reached into his fatigues and then his grandfather's cross while he whispered a prayer for guidance. In the meantime, Ramirez knew exactly where he was going.

Omega Squad and the civilian translators gathered in the middle of town and then Virgil led them down the streets toward their next destination.

The Lieutenant, Sergeant and Virgil walked ahead of the squad. It was enough space to whisper privately.

Ramirez leaned toward Virgil. "The Major back there seems to think that this is Hell. The real, Christian, fire and brimstone Hell."

Virgil smiled. "He is a great many things: Conflicted, misguided, impotent… but he is not wrong. The punishments are a little more poetic than the scriptures of man can relate."

"Shit…" Sergeant Wilson mumbled, "So what should we expect next?"

Virgil scoffed. "I am no different from those trapped here. I am bound by my position. I am only allowed to speak of things as they happen, lest I divulge someone's fate prematurely."

Wilson's face scrunched in frustration. "Listen here," he whispered and reached for Virgil's sleeve. His fingers passed through the fabric. Wilson reached again, this time his hand passing completely through Virgil's arm. "What… What do you mean by that?"

Virgil talked as if he hadn't noticed Wilson's assault. "I cannot speak of things to come." Virgil nodded back toward the rest of Omega. "If any of your soldiers were destined to meet their ends in the depths to come, then I would be remiss to alter their fate."

Lieutenant Ramirez stared straight off in the misty direction they were walking, but he felt the Sergeant's eyes—his friend's eyes—on him.

"We continue the mission," Ramirez said without hesitation.

The town disappeared behind them as Virgil led them into the mist. For a few maddeningly quiet minutes there was nothing but mist and their own bootsteps on the grass.

Then a wall appeared out of the mist, so tall that at first it looked like the other side of the cave. But it wasn't a cave, it was a gargantuan building stretching off into the mist horizontally in either direction just as it rose above them. It was made of brick with floors and floors of white-washed windows.

Directly in front of them was a single red door. Virgil pointed at it, confirming what Ramirez already knew.

Ramirez muttered a quick prayer, "Padre, dame tu fuerza, tu misericordia y tu sabiduría." It was his grandfather's and Ramirez always said the words in Spanish, just as his elder had. *Father, lend me your strength, your mercy, and your wisdom.*

From over his shoulder, Clark muttered, "We're a long way from God, sir."

The comment wasn't lost on him, but Ramirez didn't acknowledge it. Clark was an admitted atheist and Ramirez would rather keep his life vest no matter how waterlogged it was or far from shore he might be.

He gave the command and they fanned out to either side of the door in breaching positions and the Lieutenant ordered his soldiers to open it. Sergeant Wilson turned the knob and pushed it open while two soldiers filed in, rifle's leveled.

"Clear," someone called from the inside.

Then Lieutenant and the Sergeant ushered the translators and Virgil inside and followed behind them. Omega Squad congregated in the small entryway, hugging the walls. Green felt carpet lined the floor and plaster covered the walls. Orange cleaner mixed with the smell of must or mildew. There was no furniture in the entryway. The door shut behind them with a sharp clank.

Scrawled on the wall were the words:

Δώστε στον εαυτό σας. Χάνεις τον εαυτό σου. Βρείτε ότι δεν χρειάζεστε τίποτα άλλο.

Dr. Levy translated, "Give yourself. Lose yourself. You will find that you need nothing else." Dr. Levy said the words smoothly, until his voice cracked at the end. Dr. Reed stared, entranced by the writing.

The only way forward was down a long, wide hallway that stretched for hundreds of yards—green carpet receding impossibly far into the distance. Rooms dotted the hallway like a neverending hotel.

People stood in front of some of the doors. Just standing, staring at the wall opposite of their door. From what Ramirez could see, no one turned to see them enter.

The Lieutenant signaled for Omega to walk two-by-two. Utter silence, save for their own bootsteps in the hallway.

The first occupied door was a White woman, mid-thirties, dressed in business casual slacks. She didn't so much as look at them as they passed. She just stood, arms at her side, and stared at the wall across from her room, hypnotized.

Ramirez gestured again, to tell the soldiers at the rear to make sure nothing came from behind them.

They passed several more people standing outside their rooms. An Asian man in sweats, a thin Black woman in a pant-suit, a young White teen wearing swim trunks. They passed people with tattoos, tattered clothes, well-dressed and even barely dressed. Even people from different times: A tribes-woman wearing nothing but bone piercings in her nose and ears, and a grizzled sailor who stood still while the pipe in his mouth kept burning.

Every one of them motionless with the same blank stare. They all had the same nauseating hint of sulphur. In spite of that someone in the back of the squad whistled at the tribes-woman they passed.

There were some rooms in between where no one stood. With no one blocking the door, they saw writing on the doors for the first time. Each door had one thing written on it: A single name. Sounds from the room carried through the door-way and into the hall. Whispers, moaning, the steady slap of skin on skin. Twice: Angry yelling.

They passed intersections in the hallway. Each different di-rection stretching off into infinity—neverending green carpet and plastered walls and lovers waiting.

Ramirez stopped looking at them as Omega passed by.

"What are they waiting for?" Ramirez asked, remembering that Virgil was beside him. The guide walked with his hands folded in his pockets. Virgil also kept his eyes forward.

"Each is waiting for their lover. Some will wait like that for-ever never knowing who exactly they were waiting for."

The Lieutenant walked faster and the squad followed. If asked Ramirez would've blamed it on the confined spaces, but he couldn't describe the feeling of dread building in his gut. The words of the Major echoed in his head: *It's your men. Not what they will do, but what they've done.*

"Sir!" someone shouted from the back of the squad.

Ramirez whipped around, finger on the trigger of his rifle.

Sergeant Wilson was staring back at a woman. He was frozen and the entire squad was staring at him.

Ramirez walked up, grabbed his friend's shoulders and shook him. "Atticus! Snap out of it. What the fuck is the—"

Tracey was in front of the door, standing motionless. Staring at Sergeant Wilson. Ramirez's wife was wearing her pink sunflower dress, her long dark curls falling over the thick shoulders of the dress. One of her favorites. One that Ramirez hadn't seen in years—one he had forgotten about.

"It's not her," Sergeant Wilson said. "Come on, sir." Now he shook Ramirez out of it and pushed him further down the hallway.

Dumbfounded, Ramirez let himself be pushed down the hallway. He turned one last time to see the woman who looked just like his wife. She was the only one looking in their direction, watching them walk away.

It was then that the Lieutenant realized they were missing soldiers.

"Halt!" His voice echoed down the hallway. Omega Squad and the translators froze.

"Where are Turner, Harris and Lee?" he asked.

"Shit," someone mumbled.

Ramirez said, "Go back to the last intersection. Double time."

The squad jogged back the way they came. Ramirez and Sergeant Wilson kept a hand on the back of the translators,

gently pushing them along. They passed doorway after doorway, while the people standing in the hallway didn't so much
as look at them.

Except for *that* woman—the one who looked like Tracey.
She turned her head, following them as they ran down the hallway.

As they passed Tracey's look-alike, Ramirez saw the Sergeant look back over his shoulder.

"Is she following us?" Ramirez asked.

Sergeant Wilson shook his head. "No, she's just watching."

Omega stopped at the first intersection they came too. They
stared down green carpet hallways that stretched seemingly off
into the horizon. Somehow Ramirez knew they went even further than he could see and his eyes listed with vertigo.

They had passed no less than four of those intersections.
Those soldiers could be anywhere.

Lieutenant Ramirez turned toward Virgil, who looked
down the hallways with the same blank stare as the other spirits. "Where are they?"

The guide shook his head. "I am sorry."

Ramirez turned back down the hallway, back toward the
direction they needed to go. They couldn't hope to check all
the doors. Turner, Harris and Lee had to be here. They had to
be in this stretch of hallway. Otherwise they were lost.

The Lieutenant pointed to the nearest unoccupied door.
"Breach it."

Omega Squad put their backs to the wall. Sergeant Wilson
prepared to kick in the door while two others trained their rifles on the door, ready for whatever was inside. Those on the
outside of formation kept their eyes and rifles pointed down

the hallway, for they had no way of knowing how the people or spirits in the hallway would react to the intrusion.

"Breach it, but don't enter," the Lieutenant added. Silence in the hallway except for quiet moaning inside the room and the panicked breathing of the two translators.

Sergeant Wilson kicked and drove his heel hard into the door. The two sounds: The initial splintering crack of wood and the bang of the door slamming into the wall as it swung open, made even the Lieutenant wince.

"Clear," Wilson called. Then, "sir…"

Ramirez pushed past his squad.

Inside, there was only a single bedroom, the same green carpet and plaster walls as the hallway outside. The wall was seamless, without a bathroom or any other adjoining rooms. The only thing inside was a queen-size four-post bed. The sheer curtains where draped, obscuring the still-fucking couple inside. Movies played on the walls of the room like projectors were placed all around, though Ramirez could not see where the light was coming from.

Ramirez couldn't see the faces of the couple behind the curtains, but he knew immediately that neither of his soldiers were there; the man behind the curtains had dark shoulder-length hair.

He looked at the movies. Silent scenes of a family played on the walls: The same dark haired man with a blonde wife and light-haired little boy and girl. On one wall they walked across a bridge in a city. On the next wall they watched movies together on a couch. On the other, they celebrated the little girl's birthday around a kitchen lit by birthday candles.

Ramirez realized that though the long-haired man in the bed was the same as the family man from the movies, the woman in bed had dark skin and dark hair.

On the floor there were pages of hand-written notes. Ramirez stooped down and picked up a page. He recognized only one word, "amore," and guessed that the writing was in Italian or Spanish. He called back for someone that knew the language and Gomez stepped forward with the note.

"It's a love letter…" Gomez trailed off as he stared at the wall beside the entrance.

Nel fiore della passione, abbiamo trovato il nostro destino. Un'ombra d'amore all'inferno, come eravamo sopra. Lasciato morire di fame nei buchi vuoti che le nostre passioni hanno scavato.

Gomez read the words to them and his voice faltered. "In the bloom of passion, we have found our doom, A shade of love in Hell, as we were above. Left to starve in the empty holes that our passions carved."

From just outside of the hallway, Virgil said, "He will spend eternity as he did in life, dreaming and lusting after another while his life passed him by. These are images of things that might have been, had he not lost himself—"

"Enough," Ramirez said. "Breach the next door."

Again they hugged the walls while Sergeant Wilson kicked in another door. The sound echoed through the silent halls.

Each time they found the same hotel room with a couple entwined in bed while movies of another relationship or family played out on the walls. A dozen doors. Two dozen.

"We should be wasting these bastards," Miller mumbled.

"Just say the word," Davis added.

"No," Lieutenant Ramirez said. "Do not engage."

They were close again to the woman that looked like Tracey. She was still staring at Omega Squad. Watching them as they worked their way down the hallway. The only one staring at them out of hundreds of others that stood motionless.

"We should have found them by now," Sergeant Wilson said quickly. "They're not here."

"Let's get out of here," another soldier said.

Lieutenant Ramirez felt numb. Hollow. Reflexively he said, "We'll come back for them," then gestured to continue down the endless green hallway.

They jogged down the hallway.

They passed Not-Tracey and Ramirez realized that she wasn't staring at the soldiers. She wasn't staring at him. She was staring at Sergeant Wilson.

There was no doubt.

They jogged for twenty minutes before they reached the exit. For a moment, Ramirez worried they had screwed up and gotten turned around; the exit looked exactly the same as the entrance.

"If you wish to rest, you should do it now," Virgil said.

Ramirez was only vaguely aware of Dr. Levy and Dr. Reed wheezing behind him. "What's beyond the door?"

Virgil stepped forward and pushed open the door to the outside. Beyond the door was a dark muddy field with rolling hills. The sky above was black and storming a mix of rain and hail. A cold wind blew through the door, nearly taking Ramirez's breath away.

The Lieutenant sighed. "Rest for thirty minutes. Then we press on."

Ramirez leaned against the wall and slid down to the ground. He closed his eyes, just wanting to be alone for a moment. He had lost three men back there and contrary to what he said about going back for them, there was little chance they would ever be found.

He heard the shuffling of others sitting and laying around the room.

"Should—should we be worried about those things coming after us?" Dr. Levy asked.

"No," Virgil replied. "They are only there to collect a single soul. And since you're still here you need not worry about them."

"You cryptic bastard," one of the soldiers said. Definitely Miller. "It's about time you told us what's really going on."

"I cannot."

"Are those people back there?"

"No."

"Then what are they?"

Virgil didn't respond.

"Listen here you fucker—"

"Miller," Ramirez said without opening his eyes, "Do you remember how little that warlock in Africa told us? Let it go." Thankfully Miller listened.

Ramirez started to pray quietly and the rest of the squad whispered along, heads bowed. "To those who have gone before, we will carry you forward in spirit. We will mourn, but only when our call is finished. To those of us still standing, we meet our fates proudly. Amen."

There was twenty-something minutes of quiet in the alcove of that damned hotel.

Ramirez couldn't stop thinking about his squad. Turner, Harris, and Lee had all been womanizers. A different woman in every base, regardless of how many girlfriends they had back home. Sharing pictures with each other.

He thought back on what the Major said: That they were in Hell and that each circle fed on a different sin. Ramirez felt, he knew, that he would lose more men as they went deeper. They were already on par with the worst mission Ramirez had ever been on... One-by-one or two-by-two his men would succumb to their sins. How many of them would make it to Staging Area Bravo?

Ramirez kept his eyes closed, but imagined his squad and the translators sitting in the room. He thought about their sins. Where would each of his men fall? Would any of them make it?

Would he make it?

One thing—and only one thing—reassured him:

Whatever those people back there were, whatever that *thing* was wearing his wife's face, it wasn't Tracey. Tracey was alive and alright thousands of miles away.

Whatever reason that creature had for looking at Sergeant Wilson, Ramirez pushed it from his mind. His wife was fine. His best friend was fine and had made it out of the hallway with the squad. He had not succumbed to temptation as the other three had. Wilson had joked about having a thing for her, but obviously it was just that—nothing more.

Ramirez took solace in those things.

~

Dr. David Levy

David sat against the wall with Nancy, sandwiched between her and another soldier. His right leg pulsed like it was threatening to go into a cramp. He sipped on his canteen, swishing the warm metallic tasting water around his mouth to try and alleviate the dryness that had filled his mouth and throat. With any luck, it would also help with the hollow pit in his stomach.

They had just lost three men. Three men that had been standing right next to him. They hadn't cried out or reached out for anyone… They had just disappeared.

Just walked right through one of those doors.

David knew now that they were in Hell. For some reason no one wanted to come out and say it. The Lieutenant wouldn't say it. Neither would Virgil, but Virgil had slipped. He said that the people here in this hotel *lusted* after someone. David remembered the old stories about how Hell had a place for everyone based on their sins in life. Lust. Greed. Gluttony. Wrath. Fraud? Shit, what were the others?

The three soldiers had walked right through those doors. Doors made for them. To trap their souls.

And Omega Squad was going deeper.

How many circles were there? Five, seven, twenty-nine? Would they lose men at each? Would these special forces soldiers, the most capable men on the planet, slowly whittle down to nothing?

The room around David was defeaningly quiet and all he could hear was his own raspy breathing. The canteen shook as he took another sip and fumbled the cap.

What was *his* sin? What door would he disappear into?

David didn't believe in God. He was an Atheist.

Another time he might've laughed at the irony of breaking free from the childhood shackles of religion, to become a scholar whose research involved old religious texts, only to willingly walk into the depths of Hell and get trapped there for the rest of eternity. There was a joke in there, but it was hard to laugh when David felt like he was staring down the barrel of a gun.

...But Virgil said that Staging Area Alpha was filled with the souls of non-believers and Atheists. Shouldn't David have met his end in Staging Area Alpha? Had he not lived a good enough life? Should he have baked casseroles for his neighbors or tipped waiters more?

Maybe that wasn't it at all.

What was worse than non-belief? Shit, shit! What else had he done? But his mind had gone blank, as if he had never existed outside of this place. He had no way of knowing if his damning sin was in his recent life or distant past.

The thought of turning back, of running through the hotel, crossed his mind—even if no one from the squad went back with him. But who was to say that those things would let him go back out the way he came.

However many circles of Hell there were, they might as well have been chambers in a revolver. It didn't really matter that David couldn't remember, only that deep down he knew there was a bullet for him. That each circle he walked forward was another pull of the trigger.

Eating a bullet briefly crossed his mind except that suicide was a sin—a fast track to whereever he was supposed to go (or worse). He didn't want to find the proverbial bullet any quicker. So much for that.

Besides, Virgil had been right… A morbid part of David *wanted to see* what lay ahead of them.

David looked back down the infinite hotel hallway of lust with the untold souls trapped within and—the rest of him— wished that lust had been his sin. Being trapped here did not seem so bad.

He knew that every circle they walked through would be worse than the last.

~ ~ ~

The Pit

Dr. David Levy

Thirty minutes of rest for the damned. Then the Lieutenant called them to their feet and the translators were sandwiched between Omega Squad and forced through the door of the infernal hotel. It was a lot like being shoulder-to-shoulder in a subway tunnel. There was only one direction to go, and that was out onto the rolling muddy fields and into icy, pouring rain.

Dr. Levy hadn't stopped to consider the absurdity of where he was: Deep inside a cave that was so large it had its own weather. Fat raindrops and hail pelted the squad and quickly began to seep through their clothes. The fatigue he had felt inside the hotel was replaced with shock and cold.

It was nearly pitch black. The only light came from the clouds above where perpetual lightning rolled through the clouds, illuminating the hills in fragments of light. The hills themselves were a mix of mud and icy slush and slowed them considerably.

Somewhere in the distance they heard groans and screams, muffled by the falling rain and perpetual growl of rolling thunder above them.

They followed the crest of a hill, marching blindly until they came to a crest. Their hill ended and gave way to a valley—a pit. In the pit were writhing things, like huge black maggots. The pit and the creatures stretched off to the horizon in either direction.

But David heard the groans and the screams clearly now. His mouth hung open with frosty breath as he realized that the creatures were not maggots—they were people. Writhing and clambering over one another, their bodies covered in black mud, turning them into mucked silhouettes.

David, Nancy and even the soldiers recoiled at the twisted stench as it reached them. Something between death and shit and rot. David tried to think of the sulfur of the hotel—anything but what was seeping into his nostrils.

Virgil stepped forward and pointed off across the pit. Though the pit extended to the horizon to the left or right, directly across from them was another hill.

"That is where we must go," he said, raising his voice above the rain and the rumble. "We must cross the pit."

David was shaking his head feebly. He thought of the hotel—the warm hotel—and the people that stood still outside the doors. He had been terrified enough walking through those silent hallways. There didn't appear to be a way through the pit of people.

How could they cross that?

"Do not fear the creatures below," Virgil said. "They are only people."

The squad moved forward, their movements calculated and controlled compared to the chaotic scene below them. In spite of the squad and their weapons, David felt powerless, like he was a piece of seaglass about to be smashed on black rocks. A terrified piece of seaglass afraid that he might slip in the muck and mud, and be trampled beneath the soldiers feet or forgotten among the grotesque mass.

"Oh God," Nancy mumbled beside David. "Look at them."

David had been trying to think of nothing except not slipping and keeping his eyes on the soldiers in front of him. Against his judgement, he followed Nancy's gaze out into the pit—the pit they were nearly a part of.

There were mud-covered people everywhere. Their faces were caked with mud, their eyes and ears covered, so that they had to be blind and deaf to the madness around them. They clambered and flailed against each other, fighting with one another in piles that were waist and shoulder high. Some looked like they were fighting over mud and others were eating it.

In the distance, a pile of people rose up three stories, even higher than the hill that Omega had started on.

David's stomach turned and he looked away. The rumble of the thunder above was completely drowned out by groans around them. The freezing chill of the rain was reduced to a cooling downpour as the heat from the bodies built around them became unbearable.

David felt the mud churn beneath him, and he grabbed onto the nearby soldier for support. The soldier slipped an arm under his to keep him steady, but David made the mistake of looking down.

He hadn't slipped on mud. He had slipped on skin. People were buried in the mud beneath them. Twisted limbs stuck out of the ground at angles. David felt someone grab his pant leg, but he slipped free from its muddy grip.

From the piles, David heard the groans of the creatures, and as they passed, he realized they were saying one word—over and over: שלי. μου. *Mea.* Mine.

David shivered, not from the mix of ice on his shoulders and sweat on his legs, but from the terror. He walked quickly and tried to keep his eyes on the back of the soldier in front of him. Omega Squad slipped through gaps in the piles of bodies, nearly as thin as the hotel hallways. Omega moved two-by-two.

Thankfully, even the grotesque pit had periodic breaks. When he had become numb to the stench and they had walked a third of the way through, they came to a small clearing in the writhing bodies. Omega spread out, but not out of arm's reach of each other. For once, the space was not welcome and David longed for the claustrophobic steady motion of marching.

The Lieutenant was looking out over the scene with thick, night vision goggles. Around them the piles of people continued in their madness.

"Those poor dumb animals," a soldier to David's left mumbled. "Christ, look at them fighting over mud!"

Virgil added quietly, "When indulgence becomes one-sided, it becomes gluttony. Lust passes from tragic to ugly."

Another soldier asked, "Lieutenant, Sarge, where are we?"

"We're in Hell," David said, his voice surprising everyone but the Lieutenant and Virgil. "Lust, gluttony… We're passing through the circles, one by one—"

"We're going to Staging Area Bravo," the Lieutenant said. "Those are our orders."

The soldiers looked agitated for the first time; their stillness and cohesiveness was replaced by them looking away from their commander, as if each man was seeing the grotesque scene around them for the first time. David imagined that each of them had seen horrors upon horrors in their time in Omega Squad, but the realization of being in Hell was clearly different. David shuddered at the sight of seeing the soldiers unsettled, which was even worse than the scene surrounding them.

"Look at them!" the soldier called again, the same one that commented before. He stood dangerously close to a pile of scrambling people. They clambered and scooped up handfuls of mud.

He slapped the hand of the nearest creature, causing the handful of mud to plop to the ground. It wailed, it's mouth and yellow teeth clearly visible, and tried to scoop more mud.

The soldier slapped the creature's hand again and laughed at its distress. He noticed the mud caked on his hand and wiped it over the front of his uniform.

"Look at those idiots," he said.

"Young, what are you doing?" the Sergeant said.

Young let go of his rifle, letting it hang from the shoulder strap. He stooped down and grabbed a handful of mud from near the creature. "This is good stuff, Sarge." Then he rubbed the whole glob across himself. "Hah, it's mine now, you filthy fuck. Oh! This is good stuff!"

The nearest soldier to Young reached out to pull him away, but his hand slipped on Young's mud-covered sleeve. "What the fuck, Young?"

Then Young stooped down again, this time grabbing the arm of a creature and pulling it out of the writhing pile. It fell onto the ground between Young and the squad, dividing them.

"Young, stand down!" the Sergeant yelled. "That's an order."

The crazed soldier grabbed another mud-covered creature from behind and hauled it out of the pile. In a flash of lightning, David saw the soldier with mud smeared on his front and face—indistinguishable from the grotesque people around them.

"Is this how it happens?" David muttered to himself. "They go willingly. The creatures don't lash out and grab unsuspecting soldiers *or translators*..."

Soldiers were screaming now. "Young!" someone said. "I can't find him!" said another. They felt far away. "Jesus, he's gone!"

Then it sounded like thunder crashed down right on top of them repeatedly. The first blast was deafening and the others muted. David dropped to his knees and clenched his hands over his ears. It was only after it was over and he was still on the ground in the muck, that he realized one of the soldiers had opened fire. He stayed on the ground in disbelief at how loud the shots were, even while Omega Squad soldiers wrestled one another nearby. David saw, but couldn't hear the struggle because his ears were ringing.

"That's enough, Miller." The Lieutenant said in a muffled voice. "That's enough."

Slowly, the soldiers stopped struggling. Someone pulled David to his feet. When he saw it was Nancy who had pulled him up, his stomach twisted in shame. The two translators embraced each other.

"We're moving," the Lieutenant said, his voice growing louder as the ringing in David's ears faded. "Now."

Again David was pushed along, swept up in the stream of soldiers as they marched through the pit of muddy bodies. Again he thought of being a piece of seaglass, this time watching from above as they were swept through the channel. From above they were only distinguishable from the creatures around them because they were moving steadily through. They weren't trapped or wallowing or crushed beneath the weight of their sins.

David stumbled on an incline and realized that he had been keeping his eyes closed.

Omega Squad reached the other side and climbed the hill, escaping from the sweltering heat of the pit and back into the chilling rain.

David looked back over his shoulder one last time at the horrific scene they had passed through and shuddered.

~ ~ ~

The Field

Lieutenant Hector Ramirez

Ramirez led Omega Squad to the crest of the hill, the other side of the pit and didn't look back.

Above them, the sky was completely grey and covered in rolling clouds. It was impossible to tell where the sun was—if there was a sun. Light streamed in from everywhere and nowhere. As the hill leveled off, the rain stopped completely. The clouds drifted toward the pit, content to drop everything they had there. Down on the field the air was still and cold, even without the rain. Again, each of the soldiers and translators could see their breath.

Ahead of them was an open field covered in splotchy patches of grass, stretching as far and wide as the pit they left— clear into the horizon. In the distance, Ramirez could see the faint signs of movement, as patchy as the grass they walked on. It was impossible to tell from the distance, but they might have been animals or people.

Ramirez turned to Virgil, the ever-stoic guide who somehow made it out of the Pit without getting any mud on himself. He pointed across the field. "To the next Circle?"

Virgil nodded, but said nothing. He looked thoughtful or respectful. Or maybe he was keeping quiet so they didn't give away their position.

"Silence from here on out," the Lieutenant ordered. Someone in the back grumbled, probably Miller, but Ramirez let it go. The pressing concern was getting through the next Circle. At least here, Omega had enough space to give whatever those things were a wide berth.

Then he led Omega out of the rain and onto the open plains in a steady march. He didn't have time to think and couldn't give his soldiers time to think. Doubt would destroy them. They had lost four already—a third of their squad.

They would be lucky to make it to the Staging Area Bravo.

They walked for roughly three miles before the translators asked to rest.

"Five minutes," the Lieutenant replied.

Dr. Levy and Dr. Reed paced for a moment before sitting together. They leaned on each other's shoulder. Ramirez had read their files; of the two, David Levy had once before tagged along on an infiltration mission. Even that wouldn't have prepared the two translators for what they saw here.

There was nothing that *could* prepare someone for seeing the supernatural. By definition, supernatural phenomena go against rational beliefs. It was like bacteria invading a body. The only way to protect against the supernatural was to inoculate the person with a small dose of it.

Omega Squad was made that way. Each soldier, including Ramirez, was introduced to basic phenomena. Some started with parapsychology. Others were introduced to ghosts. Others, fae and cryptids. For Ramirez and Wilson, it was zombies. Slowly, each soldier was brought up to speed on "The Truth", that the world was much less simple than they had believed.

The two translators were a perfect example of why normal soldiers and civilians were not thrown into Red Level experiences without inoculation.

Somewhere up ahead was a Staging Area full of soldiers that made it through the same mess. Ramirez would be surprised if they were any better off than the translators.

The things in the distance were getting closer.

Lieutenant Ramirez pulled out his monocular and zoomed in on them. They were people, definitely humanoid, but even with the monocular it was hard to see what they were doing. To Ramirez, they looked like they might've been writhing just like the mud-covered bastards from the pit.

He scanned the horizon. In the direction they needed to go there was a mound that rose up from the horizon like a wart or a blemish. It was writhing just the same as the mound from the pit. Ramirez shuddered.

The Lieutenant continued scanning to the right—then he saw a group clearly for the first time, somewhere between a mile and a mile and half away. They were little more than silhouettes of ragged clothes, but he could tell that the people were running directly toward them.

"Move out. Double time," Ramirez ordered. Someone groaned, but no one else spoke.

Omega jogged across the field. Somewhere across there the next Circle waited for them.

"Please," Dr. Levy gasped.

"Sir," Sergeant Wilson said as he patted his CO on the shoulder.

Lieutenant Ramirez signaled for the group to halt. He pulled out the monocular again and watched the approaching group—hostiles. They were running in a full sprint and presumably had been the whole time. They were close enough now that Ramirez could see the crazed looks on their faces and the blood caked around their mouths. Their clothes were torn and covered in red and brown gore.

Five hundred yards.

"Davis," he said, still watching the hostiles. "Seven targets approaching. Remove them from the equation."

"Yes, sir." Davis stowed his M4 rifle on his back and swung his M40 sniper rifle from his other shoulder. It was an elegant piece of hardware that not only would save Omega the trouble of everyone unloading their M4s, but also had an integrated silencer that, with any luck, would keep the entire Circle from descending on them.

Davis flipped open the bipod and dropped to the ground. Within seconds his sight was calibrated and the first round tore through the air. The silencer reduced the deafening roar of the shot down to the slap of a textbook being dropped on a desk.

Lieutenant Ramirez watched the sight. The first creature in the chest, exploding in a puff of red. It dropped instantly, but writhed on the ground. The other creatures immediately turned and descended on the fallen. They were eating each other.

"Zombies. Great," Davis said. "Orders, sir?"

"Shoot another. Then we move."

There was a muffled crack as the second shot flew. As soon as the second shot connected, the creatures split their efforts between the two wounded. Davis hopped to his feet, a confidant smile on his face. He kept M40 shouldered in case a delicate, long-range touch was needed again.

Lieutenant Ramirez checked the horizon. None of the other creatures seemed to be coming toward their direction.

They marched another hour—the rest of the way to the mound in the distance. Toward the next Circle. Ramirez scanned the horizon, satisfied that they were no longer being followed. No, he was apprehensive of what they were heading toward.

The mound rose up, two stories, three stories—higher even than the one from the Pit. It was so big that there were dozens of those creatures scrambling over it and from a distance they looked like ants on an ant hill. Omega kept three hundred yards between them and circled around.

As they patched, they watched creatures clamber up and over it, pushing huge boulders back and forth. Creatures on either side, pushing against each other, trying to push the boulder over and on top of the others. Around the base, creatures fought and tore at each other, trying to steal pieces of the mountain from others.

Ramirez briefly wondered why the creatures at the top were pushing boulders, rather than eating each other, but the question was quickly forgotten when he looked closer. Looking through the monocular he was able to see just what made up the Mound.

The Mound was a red and twisted mass of body pieces, stained red with blood. The creatures were tearing away pieces, stealing them from others. The boulders at the top were boulders of people— a ball of torsos, faces and limbs mashed together like some horrific snowball.

"Greed," Virgil said. "Greed at the expense of fellow humans. Seeing them as no more than copper or gold. Humans are capable of terrible things when they see their fellows as less than human."

Ramirez shook his head. "There's no silver or gold here, Virgil. There's only people."

"To you, to us. Yes, we see people and truly there is nothing out there but people. But think of what they see."

"No," the Lieutenant replied. "I don't think I will. Move out."

Omega Squad continued their wide arc around the Mound, which kept them out of sight from the dozens of creatures that swarmed it. An hour later they had finished their arc.

"We should not dawdle here," Virgil said. "There is but one more Circle until we reach the city of Dis and your second Staging Area. There we will find respite."

Ramirez looked over his group. His squad was fine for the time being. They would make it to Staging Area Bravo. Once they got there and had to process the loss of Turner, Harris, Lee and Young… It was anyone's guess how they would manage.

At the back of the group, Smith had stopped and was staring at the ground, entranced.

"Sarge," Smith said.

Sergeant Wilson stepped forward. "What is it?"

"Do you see this?" He stooped down and picked up something off of the ground. "It's beautiful." He stood with something cupped in his hands so that no one else could see. "Jesus, Sarge…"

"What is it, Smith?"

Sergeant Wilson walked forward but when he got close, Smith staggered backward. "No, it's mine. I found it."

"I don't give a shit if you keep it, just let me see—Smith, are you fucking with me?"

"No, Sarge. Stay back. It's mine."

"Put it down! Right now."

"Smith, what are you doing, man?" Kim asked.

Omega spread out, giving the Sergeant and Smith a wide berth. It wasn't until Smith put out a hand to ward off Wilson's approach that anyone else could see what he was holding.

"Sergeant, back away from him!" Lieutenant Ramirez shouted. Wilson did.

Smith stood all alone now—the resident gambler. The squad fanned out around him. Smith was holding a bloody, severed finger. The fingertip stuck out past his glove, painted green fingernail clearly visible.

"It's mine. I found it," Smith said. He stared at it, an excited smile growing across his face. "How much do you think it's worth?"

Lieutenant Ramirez looked from Smith to the finger and back—he'd lost his mind. Ramirez asked, "What do you *think* it is, Smith?"

"It's a real, bonafide, gold coin," he said. "It's so much shinier than I thought." He turned and stared at the grisly Mound. "No wonder they're fighting over it. I thought it was a mirage. I didn't think there was any way there could be that much gold."

"It *is* a mirage, Smith," Ramirez said, trying to get him to see reason. "It's not gold. It's people, just like in the Pit back there."

"Stay back!" Smith said, his smile replaced with bared teeth. He clutched the finger to his chest. "You would say anything. You guys are just like those things! You want my gold!" Smith backed away from the group, toward the Mound.

Over his shoulder, the Mound was stirring.

Lieutenant Ramirez pulled out his monocular and looked past his crazed soldier. A group of creatures from the mound were running toward them—all of them, save for the ones at the top who refused to let go of their boulders.

Smith turned and ran toward the Mound—toward the creatures.

"Smith, no!" Kim yelled and started to run, but two other soldiers tackled them to the ground. "Smith!" he yelled from the ground.

The entire squad watched in stunned silence as Smith ran almost all the way toward the creatures. He only turned at the last second and ran to Omega Squad's path, as if realizing that the creatures were just as greedy.

"Davis, drop two, please."

"Waste 'em," Miller sneered.

Ramirez watched through the monocular as the muffled shots rang out. Two creatures crumpled to the ground in a puff of red mist. As soon as they did, the creatures stopped and turned on their wounded friends, beating them and biting off chunks of flesh.

Ramirez watched, stunned, until Smith fell on one of the wounded and started biting their arm. He nearly dropped the monocular to the ground. "Let's get the fuck out of here."

Davis shot once more before standing. Ramirez didn't have to ask who it was for.

~ ~ ~

The Parlor

Dr. David Levy

They walked for another mile across the barren fields of Greed.

To David, it felt like eternity. The sky above them was covered in clouds and the sun seemed to hang in the sky. They had to have been walking for hours, but time didn't hold any meaning down here. David's legs were stiff and were beyond sore. They were numb, and felt swollen with blood and lactic acid.

Not even the city of Dis rising in the distance made him feel better.

"Dis is the centrum of the underworld," Virgil said, talking loud enough for all the squad to hear. "All other circles lay within it. Not much longer now. Another half mile or so and we will reach the river, Styx."

David and Nancy were in the center of the squad again. Now that there were no more enemies, no more danger, Omega Squad had spread out. Each soldier was more than an arm's length away from the others. David and Nancy were the only two that walked beside each other.

The Sergeant asked, "Will we be meeting another boatman, like the first one we crossed? Anchor? Akeron?"

"Acheron," Virgil corrected calmly. "And no. There are no boatmen to ferry us across the Styx. We must go underneath it, through the next Circle of Hell."

"What's the next Circle?" Nancy asked. In spite of her breathing and soreness, she had kept it together remarkably well. David glanced at her with newfound admiration. Was there nothing that she couldn't do?

"The next Circle houses the sin of Wrath. The denizens of Hell call it the Parlor."

"That doesn't sound so bad," Nancy said.

David muttered, "Troubling—considering all the names have sounded pretty damn harmless so far: The Pit, the Field. Does the Parlor have any other names?"

Virgil turned and walked backwards for a moment while he answered, a smile on his face. "Why yes, good scribe. Those who dwell inside that Circle call it the dungeon. But in all actuality, it is Hell by any other name."

The City of Dis rose over the horizon like spiked suns. The towers of the city spanned the horizon and were impossibly, blindingly white. David had to squint and cover his eyes to look at them.

Before the spires rose so high and threatened to completely blind Omega, they came upon the brackish green waters of Styx. The river seemed to blot out all the glare from the spires.

The contrast between the bright pillars and dark river gave the appearance of a black and white sunrise.

Rather than approaching the river, Virgil diverted them off to the right, parallel to Styx for several minutes as he searched for something. Soon he found it: A small stone stairway that zig zagged down five flights to a small cavern. Omega Squad flicked on red flashlights. The air grew cold and the stones were moist. David clutched the outcroppings of rock to steady his poor legs.

The final flight of stairs opened up to a two-story tall door. It was half collapsed, metal rebar jutted out from the concrete at odd angles.

Rather than using the door, Virgil led them over to a waist-high hole in the concrete and crawled through it. Before David could ask for a break, the Lieutenant and Sergeant and several soldiers followed the guide through. Then it was David's turn and on shaking hands and knees he crawled through.

Inside, they were in a hallway of sorts, lined with concrete and jagged rebar. The squad walked single file. David was reminded of the cave as he followed the soldier in front of him and caught ghostly red flashes of the trail ahead. They ducked under collapsed walls and even crawled in multiple places.

Then they heard the screams.

Somewhere on the other side of the concrete to the left they heard low-pitched howls, like apes rather than wolves. The squad stopped and waited. Then they heard several howls in quick succession, followed by bangs and thumps and rapid, heavy footsteps.

Then something crashed against the wall, the impact reverberating through the concrete and shaking the tight confines around them. Dust and soot fell and turned the room into fog. David and Nancy crouched down.

Beyond the wall came more howls of creatures. Then an ape-like scream. A squish. Heavy footsteps receding. Silence.

Omega Squad stood still for what felt like minutes. The dust had settled and no more sounds came from the other side of the wall.

Finally, they continued their shuffling through the tight hallway of the Parlor.

In the red light of the crushed hallway they climbed through two more narrow passageways.

All the while heavy footsteps fell intermittently on the other side of the wall. They came in sets, as if some large creature paced on the other side—paced and paused. Every few minutes an inhuman howl and the building would shake with violence.

David's legs felt like gelatin now and his calves and thighs burned with every step. He reached out for every handhold of the broken wall or exposed rebar to steady himself. He was terrified of whatever lay beyond the walls and that kept him moving.

But a part of David wanted to sit down here, in relative safety, and never get back up. He could live out the rest of his life in the darkness. Even when Omega Squad left, the flashlight ran out and he jabbed himself on exposed rebar trying to navigate the hallways, that fate was preferable to whatever horrors lay outside or… in deeper Circles of Hell.

That was it, wasn't it? David was thousands of miles from home, in some desert in the Middle East. But he wasn't really there anymore either. He was through the Doorway, across the river, Acheron, and across three (or four) Circles of Hell. But being that far from home, from safety, wasn't the worst of the things that weighed on David Levy's mind.

The worst was that somewhere down here in the coming despair, was the Circle where David would be caught by his own sin, like a squealing rabbit in a trap. He would die down here and he would suffer for all eternity.

So the idea of staying like a leper in this crumbling hallway of the Parlor didn't seem so bad. Maybe he could learn the hallways so that he could become a guide like Virgil. Then he could guide others deeper into Hell, toward Circles he was too terrified to visit.

In the darkness David smiled at the absurd idea.

The thought of hiding in the darkness of the hall didn't last. They found writing on the wall. Whoever had done it had probably used rebar to etch into the concrete, but something about the writing gave David the mental image of the author scrawling it into the walls with their fingernails.

One scrawled in Latin, *Habere amisit omnia, nisi odium meum,* translated to *I have lost everything except my hatred.*

Another in English: *The Parlor is lovely, dark and deep. It's not so bad. Except for JOHN. I'LL FUCKING KILL HIM.* The last words scrawled in towering letters as if they'd been slashed into the wall.

Thoughts of whatever had scrawled those messages lurked just beyond his vision. David began to dread every blind section of the hall.

Up ahead, light for the first time. Beams streamed through cracks in the wall. The Lieutenant and the Sergeant paused at the openings to look through, studying whatever lay beyond.

Behind them, Virgil's sharp features were illuminated in the red light of a flashlight.

Omega Squad continued forward, creeping along. David kept glancing between his feet, and toward the opening; afraid to trip and yet his curiosity overcame his fear. Each soldier paused only briefly to look out. When it was David's turn, he held his breath.

Beyond the wall was a huge, multi-leveled concrete room. It was gray, save for streaks of dark red, dried blood. Some sections stretched as high as four stories tall, others were alcoves as small as a single story. Stairs wrapped around the outer walls, leading to different rooms and balcony areas. Light shown starkly and unevenly.

Littered around the room were boxes made from the same concrete as the rest of the room. The boxes were arranged in clusters and gave David the eerie impression that those were sitting areas, and the boxes were tables and chairs. To the right was an arrangement that might've been a cubist arrangement of a bar and barstools.

On the boxes were people… but they were all wrong.

A man lumbered through the room, so tall that he could look over the second story of the room. But it wasn't his immense height that made David gasp, it was the rest of his proportions. The man's muscles and shoulders and limbs were ballooned and elongated, to the point that he looked more like an ape than a man. He was naked aside from the scraps of cloth that hung around his ankles. His skin was stretched thin to the point of being not just pale, but blue and red from the tissues beneath it—it was even torn around the joints and scabs caked the creature's elbows and shoulders. Its face was even more twisted: Tusks grew up from the bottom lip and jutted up in front of its cheeks. Its eyes were so bloodshot that all that was left was red and a black dot of a pupil.

The man-creature lumbered past several others that reclined on the concrete chairs. Each stared intently with their red eyes, but the first creature waddled past and sat on an empty section of block.

"Keep moving," a soldier whispered from behind David, causing the translator to jump.

He shuffled down the crumbled hallway after the rest of the Omega.

They passed another opening in the hallway, one with barely any light showing through. This time a creature was trapped within a tiny concrete room. It was hunched over, arms folded around its body, almost as if the room had shrunk around it, trapping the creature—or it had grown so large that it had trapped itself.

Beady red eyes stared back through the breaks in the wall and David shuddered even though the creature was utterly trapped. It snorted at David, but its breath was weak and feeble within the confines.

Omega Squad walked through most of the Circle of Wrath in the red light of their flashlights with only the occasional howls of violence from beyond the walls.

Until the imps found them.

First came cackling from somewhere in the twisted rebar above their heads. David hadn't thought to look up until then. He realized that the thin hallways they walked stretched upward for several stories. It was then that he realized they were not inside a hallway—they were inside the walls of the Parlor, like rats trying to avoid being squashed.

The cackling, and occasionally a creak or groan of rebar, followed above their group for what felt like an hour to David.

"Do not pay them any mind," Virgil said, just loud enough for Omega to hear. "They are other denizens of Wrath, but they are cowards. They will not harm you."

David felt a rain of rocks on his head and shoulders, just enough to remind him that they were being followed.

"They're lucky they aren't down here with us," a soldier said from behind David.

Light poured into the hallway from somewhere up ahead. The heavy footsteps and howls of creatures echoed. The Lieutenant slowed even further and crept until they came to a complete opening in the wall, drowning out their red lights. He peeked out around the wall.

"We will need to walk the outer rim," Virgil said. "It is only for a moment and then we will be back in the safety of the hallway."

There was a rumble that shook the walls. The entire Parlor quaked all around them. The Lieutenant held up his hand, a sign David recognized as "hold".

A few seconds later the Lieutenant turned to the squad. "Virgil is right. We can follow the edge of the wall to another opening and be back in the dark in no time."

Something swept by David's head, causing him and the rest of the squad to duck. He looked up and saw one of the imps staring back at the squad. It was small, and only vaguely resembled a person—twisted much the same as the gorilla-people, except that it was smaller and resembled a monkey. Its skin sagged, as if it had shrunken while its skin stayed the same.

Flaps hung loosely on its arms and legs, and were torn in scabbed strips in several places. Where this was from the rebar or other creatures, David could not guess. The skin of its face sagged so much that it looked like it was melting off; the white of its skull showed beneath its eyes and on its lower lip.

The creature was smiling at them when it spoke in a giggling, hyena voice. "Little soldier brats, little soldier brats, see how they run. See how they run. Look at their guns. Look at their guns. Come have some fun."

"Permission to engage?" the soldier said from behind David.

"No, Miller," the Lieutenant said. "Not with all those creatures outside."

The imp above them smiled even wider and cackled, seeming to delight in the dread that was spreading across David's face.

"We are leaving," the Lieutenant said. "Single file. Quickly and quietly. Do not engage with the creatures outside. Make sure the translators don't fall behind."

David forced himself to look away from the horrid creature and to the soldier in front of him. Then Omega Squad took off out of the safety of the hallway and into the light. In spite of the urgency, David couldn't help but look at the space beyond.

The room outside was gigantic and the sheer size made David gasp. He tried to glance between the room and the soldier in front of him, and in those brief times could only guess that the room rose up five or six stories. It was the same sheer concrete as the others, but the floor and ceiling were bowed and cracked. Everyone walked close to the wall, staying away from the steep slope of the collapsed floor in the center of the room.

Above, the river Styx leaked through the ceiling in a steady downpour and collected into a chasm on the floor below.

A behemoth of a creature took up a third of the room. It sat on the ground and was so tall that even as it sat, its shoulders were rounded and its tongue reached the ceiling as it lapped greedily at the pouring waters of the Styx. The gorilla creature's skin was completely gone, its muscle and tendons and bones were scabbed with blood and puss. Its tusks were ground down into stubs from where they rubbed against the concrete ceiling as it lapped at the leaking river.

All around it were dozens of other creatures, and even though they were two or even three stories tall, they looked like toys compared to the behemoth. Their skin hung in patches. The creatures lapped at the brackish green waters that collected in the collapsed floor.

Omega Squad followed the outer wall and went back inside the next crack in the wall. Back inside to the safety of the hallway.

David was nearly inside when a fight broke out between the creatures below. Several of the largest creatures turned, pummeling and slashing at each other. Howling mad.

David slipped on the gently sloping concrete, but thankfully the soldier in front and behind him reached out and grabbed his vest. David stood quickly and shuffled with the squad.

Across the room the behemoth waved a hand in an almost gentle sweep of the commotion beside it, like it was brushing away flies. For such a gentle motion it was devastating to the room around it. Its hand was bigger than all the other creatures and when it collided with them, snapping bones echoed like gunshots through the room. A dozen creatures were thrown halfway across the gigantic room. Those that fell into the pool of brackish water slipped below its surface without struggling. Those that collided with other creatures were ganged up on and beaten to death when they landed.

Then David slipped back into the hallway, lit only by the red light from Omega's head lamps. The howls and screams continued for only a moment. When they stopped, Omega was left with only the sounds of their shuffling feet and the cackling of the imps above them.

The imps continued in their hyena voices, "Little black brats, clutch your guns tight. Don't catch a fright. Don't catch a fright."

Beaten to death, he thought uneasily. But could anything really die in Hell? David smiled out of equal parts absurdity and fear.

Omega Squad pushed forward through the dusty, jagged hallway, spurned onward by Virgil maintaining that they had passed fully underneath the river Styx. He said they were nearing the end of the Parlor and the entrance to the city of Dis.

The howls and sounds of death still echoed occasionally through the walls and the imps pestered them from above, but they didn't come down. The imps were content with insulting them from above.

"Little black brats," they cackled. "Little black brats, watch how they cry. Listen to them lie. Watch how they die." The lines echoed through the walls, vying for David's attention. Try as he might to focus on the soldier in front of him, on dodging the rebar spikes and on not tripping, he couldn't help but hear the imps.

He wasn't the only one having trouble.

Miller, a soldier behind David, was having trouble staying quiet against the imps' comments.

"Come on down, little shits. I've got two knives, one for each of you. Come on down."

The imps cackled back with, "See the little angry pus. He is not so different from us."

"Can I shoot them, Lieutenant?"

David watched as the ceiling above him was illuminated by a barrel-mounted red flashlight. Even though he knew he shouldn't, David looked up, just in time to the horrid, sagging face of an imp staring back at him—smiling. It's bottom lip drooped completely off of its teeth and lower jaw. Its face was so slumped that the only reason David knew it was smiling was that the upper lip was somehow still attached.

The worst was their incessant smiling.

"No," the Lieutenant said. "Do not engage."

Then one of the imps swung down and Nancy screamed somewhere behind David.

"Ow! Help!" she screamed.

"Shit, get it off," another soldier said.

David ducked instinctively and turned to see one of the imps hanging from a ledge by one hand and with the other it was pulling on Nancy's hair. Then the creature squealed in pain, let go and hauled itself back up to the floors above. Blood dripped down onto Nancy's head and shoulders.

Miller was holding his knife. "Serves you right!"

More imps swung down, swiping gnarled hands and feet at Omega Squad as they passed overhead, highlighted in the red glow of flashlights.

Then thunder rang out from the back of the squad. David recognized the sound of gunfire immediately. Miller had opened fire on their assailants—against orders. For a few seconds, David screamed but he couldn't hear it over the shots.

David watched with half-closed eyes as Imps dropped from the rafters above. One nearly fell on David—it bounced off a nearby outcropping and landed on the ground beside him. Its arms twitched against David's foot.

For a few brief seconds of deafening silence, all was calm. Someone hauled David to his feet and pushed him further down the hallway.

Then the wall behind him exploded. David hadn't heard it—he had *felt* it.

He turned to see a hole where a wall should've been, a tree trunk of an arm reaching through, and a huge, red and white hand wrapped around Miller. The soldier's mouth was open in an angry scream. He stabbed the hand over and over with his knife.

Then he was gone; the creature pulled Miller through the wall like a toy.

David watched the soldiers in the back of the squad open fire. Muzzles flashed and the only thing he heard was the distant sound of thunder.

Someone grabbed his vest collar and hauled him forward, away from the chaos. Further into the darkness. They ran in red light and silence.

Somewhere behind them the hallway exploded again and again as creatures punched through, trying to get them. The imps stopped following them and stayed to heckle their attackers, their voices sprinkled in between the breaking concrete.

"Big dumb brutes. Missed me—you missed me."

Thankfully, they left the chaos behind after a few minutes of terrified running. Then David went back to stumbling on numb legs instead of fearing for his life.

~ ~ ~

The City of Dis

Dr. David Levy

Later, when David had lost track of how far they ran or how long they had been in darkness—just as his hearing was coming back—Omega reached the end of the Parlor.

They passed through one last opening in the broken slabs of concrete and rebar, and exited to a set of stairs much like the ones they had walked down to get into the Parlor. Again, David was afraid they had gotten turned around.

His mind was set at ease after they walked up the flights of stairs and came into the open air again—and the city of Dis stood before them in its blinding glory. The walls were sheer stone, completely smooth without any brick lines at all—as if the entire wall had been chiseled from a singular piece of stone. Now that they were so close the size was staggering; the entire wall was as high as a skyscraper. David craned his neck and nearly fell over trying to see the tops of the towers that lined the wall. Off to either side, the castle walls stretched out to the horizon.

"The city of Dis," Virgil narrated as they walked. "A wall between the outer and inner Circles of Hell. Your second Staging Area lies within."

Ahead of them were two giant golden doors. Equally large pictures are etched on them of wings and fire and symbols that David did not recognize. As Omega craned their necks to look at the doors, Virgil narrated.

"The doors to Dis depict the fall of Lucifer and his angels. At the top of the door, where the light is blinding and mortals cannot see lies the etchings of the Argument and Lucifer's Rebellion. What lies at the top of your vision is the Fall." The top half of the doorway was obscured by the blinding light reflecting off the castle wall.

Halfway down, where Omega could finally see, hundreds of angels, clumps of wings, were depicted falling down the doors and came to rest two stories up. "Down here you see the etchings of the city of Dis and the beginnings of the Circles." The bottom etchings of the doorway (the smallest part in regards to the whole) were the ornate rings of Hell. As David and the others neared the doorway they started to see the exquisite detail in each ring. There were even tiny etchings of sufferers in each ring—

—and they were moving. It was so slight that it might've been a trick of the mind, but David knew that down here that the stranger of the explanations was true.

The absurd thought crossed his mind that if he stared in just the right spot of the etching of the city of Dis that he would see Omega Squad bunched around the gates. Maybe he would even see his own tiny, weary self.

Then thunder rumbled above them, dangerously close, as if it was rolling down the golden doors. The entire Squad recoiled.

Two creatures descended on either side of the gates, each vaguely in the shape of a winged human. Each leg was the size of a tree trunk. Colossal feet touched the ground and David braced for a quake, but none came. As the massive wings beat, no sound or wind came with them.

Omega Squad backed away, weapons trained on the creatures. Even Virgil stumbled backward.

Both creatures had huge, hoofed feet. David looked steadily up and saw that each had two sets of wings. One set was crossed over their bodies, hiding their torsos and arms, while the other set was folded behind their backs. Their feathers and skin were mottled grey and brown. Both creatures easily stood three stories tall, their shoulders higher than the etchings of the rings of Hell on the golden doors.

Their faces looked human at first but as David stared he saw that their faces alternated between human and animal, flashing back and forth like a flipbook. The creature on the left had the face of an ox-man and the one on the right had the face of a lion-man.

Virgil stepped forward, comically dwarfed by the two creatures. "It is I, Virgil, come to guide more mortals through the gates. Stand aside and let us pass.

Again thunder boomed and the sound startled the humans and guide alike. Even though the creatures remained perfectly still, now it was clear that the rumblings came from them and were the language of the creatures.

When the air was quiet again, Virgil replied with, "We shall see."

The squad stared at the creatures and the creatures stared off somewhere above them, seemingly looking over the outer Circles of Hell. In spite of that, David could *feel* their gaze. It was as if they didn't need their eyes to see or their wings to fly—as if the strange form they took now wasn't their true form.

When the silence became unbearable and David's heart was beating in his ears, the sky above flashed. David turned, looked up and then fell frightened to the ground.

A third, terrible creature had appeared in the sky above them. Overwhelming and barely comprehensible. Six brilliant-white wings stretched out in a dozen directions, so enormous they stretched off into the horizon and blotted out the sky. One set of wings was folded across the body of the beast, nearly covering it all. From the small sections of body that remained, David saw whirring golden gears, each as large as the rings of Hell.

From the new creature erupted a sound that was as far from thunder as thunder was from a gunshot—so deafening that David wasn't sure if he had heard anything at all.

As suddenly as it had appeared, the terrible creature was gone and the sky was a barren, cloudy grey. When David blinked he saw the blurry afterimage of gold and white burned into his eyes.

Behind them, the other creatures guarding the city had backed away from the golden doors. The doors were open and the city of Dis lay beyond.

"Come quickly," Virgil said. Though he was shouting, his voice was barely a whisper.

David stumbled along with Omega into the city of Dis.

The city was the same eerily smooth white stone as the outside. Virgil led them onward mercilessly onto the wide, barren mainstreet. Hard edges and empty windows surrounded them. There wasn't a soul to be seen.

At first, David wasn't sure if he was completely deaf and maybe couldn't hear the sounds of people hiding behind the walls, like those twisted people of the Parlor. It wasn't until he heard his own sullen footsteps and those of Omega Squad that he realized they were completely alone in the city.

As if sensing his question, Virgil said, "We are nearly there. Do not be afraid of the silence. The only beings here are those of your military, unafflicted and unpossessed."

David asked weakly, "What were those things at the gate?"

The Lieutenant called back over his shoulder, "You don't want to know."

"Yes, yes I do."

Virgil responded plainly, "Those *things* were angels."

David had long since thought his legs would give out. They had passed from pain to numbness, back and forth, a dozen times; he could not tell which was worse. Somewhere in the back of his mind loomed the horror of the Circles he had crossed but the pain in his legs quieted even the horrors, muting them to radio static.

Though his eyes flitted between the barren streets, countless empty windows and his own feet, occasionally he glanced at the soldiers. They looked just as broken and empty as David felt. David wasn't sure whether that was comforting or horrifying that men such as them were as scared as he was.

Virgil kept them all moving. The guide walked unerringly and undeterred by the horrors they had witnessed. Maybe he was as numb as the rest of them and just hid it better.

The City of Dis felt like a desert around them instead of the salvation that David had imagined. The white walls were bare. There were no placards or tapestries anywhere in the city.

Then they found the first signs of life. Three soldiers kept watch out in front of a nondescript building. They stared at the newcomers in disbelief, before hollering something into the building. A lone soldier stumbled forward. His uniform was clean, but he had days-old bags under his eyes and a defeated look in them. With effort he stood up straight and saluted the Lieutenant.

"Omega Squad reporting," the Lieutenant said. "We are in need of a place to rest and I need to speak to your CO."

The soldier half-smiled at that, as if he understood all too well what Omega had just passed through. "Right this way, sir." The other two soldiers on guard nodded to the squad as they passed.

Again, David expected salvation and was denied.

Inside was the same barren stone as outside, except now the stone was arranged as furniture about a room: Stone couches, stone chairs and stone table. Twenty or thirty soldiers sat or lay on the ground. Some were fortunate enough to have thin sleeping bags. A couple of the men glanced their direction when they entered, but none of them saluted or even greeted the newcomers.

The two groups stood in uneasy silence before the Lieutenant broke it.

"Stay here. Rest. I'll ask the CO about accommodations."

"In here, soldier," called a gruff voice from a nearby room. And with that the Lieutenant was gone, leaving his squad of broken men with equally broken company.

David listened to the footsteps of the Lieutenant and CO of the Staging Area recede into the distance. The soldiers that were left didn't speak, except that a few from Omega wept quietly.

David and Nancy sat side by side against the far wall, leaning against each other's shoulders and whispering quietly amongst themselves.

"Some salvation," David said. "They look as bad as us."

"I thought this was going to be a vacation," Nancy said wistfully. "You know, not the actual mission... I had plane tickets to Dubai. I was supposed to meet Bret and Aliz. Shit, they are probably wondering where I am."

"You shouldn't curse," David said. "You're liable to get stuck here."

Nancy smiled. Somehow that was enough to kindle a small flame against the overwhelming despair.

"I had papers I was going to write, you know," Nancy said. "Three that I was working on." She held up fingers for emphasis. Then her smile dropped. "Do you ever regret your work?"

David shook his head. "Of course not. Even if there was a flaw in the premise, I could always fix it. I try not to regret work already done. Now if you're talking about those papers you haven't gotten too—then yes, I concur and I agree.'

This time she didn't smile at his joke. David watched and waited for her to elaborate. What could she possibly regret about her work? Dr. Nancy Reed was a pillar of ancient history. Moreover, she was one of David's professional inspirations. Seeing Nancy talk about her work like that was almost as unsettling as the Hells they had passed through.

"I—I have regrets," she finally said. "Some of my papers... Well, the easy way to say it is that I didn't treat my colleagues as well as I should have. I reaped a lot of credit for their work."

"Don't do that to yourself," he replied. It was commonplace for lead researchers to have their names placed above their assistants. "I'm sure that having your name attached helped their career enough. Besides, if every bad boss wound up in Hell then this place would be full."

Nancy's lip quivered, but she forced a smile as she said, "We're not going to make it are we?"

~

Lieutenant Hector Ramirez

The man in charge of Staging Area Bravo was Captain Dawson, a man just as worn and tortured as the rest of his soldiers. His beard was ragged and the front of his uniform was torn where he had ripped off his ribbons and medals.

Captain Dawson led Ramirez out of the building and didn't let them speak until they were half a dozen blocks away from the others. Still, he looked over his shoulder every few seconds. Ramirez couldn't tell if it was because the Captain thought they might be followed or that he thought there might be dangers lurking in this concrete wasteland.

"So, Command sent more of you poor bastards our way, huh? I thought they would pause after the Major didn't make it, but then I remembered no one's gone back to tell them." The Captain's voice was as hoarse as his face was weary. He pulled out a crumpled pack of cigarettes and lit one without offering another to Ramirez.

The Lieutenant nodded.

"Well, that's all fine and good. Seeing as how we're stuck here. Command sends ten men, one makes it through to Bravo. Exchange rate is shit, but it doesn't much matter when you're just the one writing the checks—not your money, not your neck." Dawson paused and half-smiled, as if he was expecting a laugh. Ramirez didn't have it in him.

"Sir, what's inside the city?"

The Captain took a drag. "Fuck the pleasantries, am I right?"

Ramirez waited.

"What's inside the city? The rest of Hell, that's what. The *other* sins."

"Go on."

The Captain looked off into the city suddenly, looking for some imagined threat. A few seconds later he answered, "I don't know. I didn't exactly go to Sunday school and that guide, Virgil, he's about as worthless as the rest of Command. I contemplated torturing him to get him to talk, but he's already dead, so there's that."

Davis and Gomez were probably contemplating the same thing. Lot of good it would do them.

"What's the mission, sir?" The Lieutenant asked.

Dawson looked at him, his face turned in a question.

"The mission was to get here. I assumed the mission was to go deeper. To go to the center."

Dawson stared off into the city now. Not looking at any particular point, but looking through it—a thousand miles away.

"That was always the mission," the Captain said. "Get to the center... Fuck. You know, after the Major didn't make it here... I tried to be the type of commander that *knew* what he was asking of his boys. I tried to feel each and every loss, tried to remember what it was like when artillery dropped nearby or an IED went off down the street. But I was lying to myself. I was so far away. So far away." Dawson turned to Ramirez. "Let me tell you, *I'm here* now. I've seen the shit. I know what the mission is, and I say fuck them. I won't order my men to go any further. Lieutenant, you and your men are on your own."

We are always alone, he thought. Ramirez stared at the broken Captain. He didn't feel shock or rage—he just felt pity.

Ramirez wasn't going to get anything worthwhile out of Dawson. Any rest he and his men got in this barren city wasn't going to be enough to alter the mission they were on.

What the Captain *hadn't said* was just as important as what he had said. They were still here, still at Bravo. They hadn't defected. Which meant that they were terrified of going back through the former circles or that some of them had already tried.

The Lieutenant turned around and started walking back to the Staging Area. The Captain walked with him without protest. The only sounds were their footsteps and an occasional loud drag on a cigarette.

"I'm sorry," the Captain said sometime later, flicking the butt off into the street. "I wish I could help you. I really do. I'm sorry," he repeated.

Ramirez shrugged; he didn't have anything else to say. Dawson didn't speak again until the soldiers and Staging Area came back into view.

"I guess most of us were going to wind up here eventually. Hell, if Command would've waited a little while longer than they would be here too. Then they could see it for themselves."

Back with the soldiers, the Captain went into his office and came out with a bundle of papers. They were loosely bound with string and so old and faded that bits cracked off as the Captain handed them to Ramirez.

"Here. Might be something. We found it on the way in. There's not much else around."

Lieutenant Ramirez carefully looked through the pages, but they were all written in a language vaguely familiar but that he didn't know.

"Thanks," he said absently and walked back out into the main area, stepping over and around soldiers laying on the floor. He sat at the lone table in the room and called for Dr. Levy and Dr. Reed.

"What do you make of this?" he asked, gently setting the papers in front of them.

Both translators sat down with heavy eyes.

"Well, this is Latin," Dr. Reed said as she delicately turned the pages. "This… this might be Italian back here."

Ramirez called for Gomez, who sprung up and jogged over to the table.

Dr. Reed said, "This is poetry, or notes of some kind." She mumbled the beginning of the Latin phrase, "*Noli timere… Do not be afraid; our fate cannot be taken from us.*"

Dr. Levy read over her shoulder, "*I found myself within a dark woods where the straight way was lost…*"

Dr. Reed again, "*The stars are starting to fall away*—Oh, here at the bottom—*I shall write in my native tongue for it is my choice and not my charge.* That's where the Latin ends."

Gomez leaned in close and silently looked over the other pages in Italian. "He rewrote some of the same stuff. It's—it's all poetry. *The stars are starting to fall away and we are not permitted to stay.*" He gestured for the next page. "Lots of rhymes… *Hell is both far older and… It was already there before the beginning, before the Lord, waiting, and its abyssal hunger knows no sating.*"

"That doesn't make any sense," Ramirez said. "Hell didn't come first."

Dr. Levy pointed to a large section and though Ramirez couldn't read the text, it was all the same phrase, repeating over and over for an entire page.

Gomez scanned the entire page, mumbling to himself before repeating the phrase aloud. "*Hell is made of fire and ice.* That doesn't make sense. That's all it says. There's nothing here, sir. Not even a name on any of the pages."

Ramirez sunk a little in his chair and glanced around the room. All the soldiers were quietly lounging around. Even Virgil was leaning against the wall. He must have been somewhere else, thoughtfully. If Virgil had been listening to their translation, the guide didn't offer any insights—Ramirez suspected that even if he was, Virgil wouldn't help them.

Lieutenant Ramirez and Sergeant Wilson sat across the street against one of the bare walls of the concrete prison-city. They shared a canteen of water between them. Ramirez wasn't even thirsty, but thought that he should drink anyway.

Something like twelve hours had passed—a soldier's guess-timation but you wouldn't know it from the wristwatches that had all stopped or from the sky. It was the same unchanging gray, cloud-covered mess. The clouds didn't even look like they were moving. An impossible sky inside a cave that shouldn't exist. Ramirez and the others managed to get a few hours' sleep, but in that time many of them looked just as ragged as the soldiers stationed in the city.

The two friends watched the soldiers on guard scan the city, knowing that there wasn't another soul to be found within, human or devil.

"I wonder if the Bears are playing today," Wilson said.

"Probably losing," Ramirez replied with a chuckle.

It was the kind of B.S. back and forth they always had on a mission. When the air was heavy and thick with danger, the conversation was light in response. If they had been back on base in safety they might've talked about family instead.

Ramirez said, "I wonder what book Tracey's reading now."

"You know it's something horrible."

"Oh, they're not so bad—or at least it's not so bad hearing her talk about them."

His friend hung his head at that, like there was something he wanted to say, but couldn't bring himself to say. Ramirez nudged his friend.

"Alright, alright," Wilson said. He took a deep breath. "Remember when you thought Jordan swiped those heart cookies your mom mailed?"

Ramirez punched his friend in the shoulder. "Yeah, that was back in Basic. You ate them. Get out of here—you confessed the day after it happened."

Wilson cracked a smile.

"You never could keep a secret," Ramirez added.

The smile on Wilson's face was short-lived. Ramirez might have chalked it up to something he said, except that they were literally in Hell.

But then the location wasn't the only thing different about this mission. A quiet tear ran down the Lieutenant's cheek. They had never lost so many men. One, sure—those hurt. Ramirez remembered each and every man he lost under his command. Mourned each and every man. He visited their families, spoke to their wives and children or their parents. It was easy when it was one at a time.

Losing half of his squad was incomprehensible. It was something like getting shot—worse... Ramirez had been shot before. The bullet broke the ceramic plate in his vest and broke a rib too—it sucked. But he had read about guys getting riddled with bullets and still fighting. Of course most of them died, but survivors of trauma like that said they didn't even feel the pain. It was like their body shut down those receptors. The body could only feel so much.

Since they had entered Hell, the number of soldiers lost under Lieutenant Ramirez's command had doubled. He didn't feel sad. He didn't feel the loss of so many. Ramirez felt numb. Numb like someone riddled with bullets. Someone who experienced so much trauma that the only thing keeping them going was pure adrenaline. Someone who was just holding off dying a little longer.

"The only reason they survived is because they're still here," Ramirez said with clarity.

"What are you on about?" Wilson asked.

"The soldiers here. They haven't met their sin yet. That's why they're still here."

Wilson paused, as if he was considering what his friend said. "They're all damned, huh? So if all the Circles of Hell get worse and worse the further in we go... then you think that there's nothing but horrible men here. Horrible people that haven't made it to their Circle yet?"

"Something like that."

"There's good men in there too."

"I don't think the good men made it this far."

Wilson scoffed. "Bullshit. I know at least one good one that made it."

Ramirez glanced over and saw his friend's look. "I know you're not talking about me."

He was. The Sergeant glanced down. "Well, consider the alternative: If there's nothing but horrible people that made it this far… What does that say about us?"

That question haunted Ramirez for the rest of his time in the city of Dis. Lieutenant Ramirez gave them a full eight hours to sleep though only a handful could sleep that long. There was something about being down there that affected their needs to eat and sleep. Other squads would chalk it up to the perpetual daytime or to the horrors they witnessed on their way. Neither by themselves was the whole story, though they were likely pieces of the whole story.

It was simple *being* there, inside a supernatural realm.

The human body was developed for many things: A regular, twenty-four hour day, four seasons, roughly two thousand calories a day, and so on. Supernatural realms were not made for people and the human body was extremely sensitive to being outside of the real plane of existence.

It wasn't healthy to spend prolonged periods inside a supernatural realm. Even with Omega Squad's training, their longest mission was only five days. Those five days had strained his men to their limits.

Hell might do the same in half the time. It had likely only been twenty hours since they passed through the Doorway. They were only halfway to the center.

The Lieutenant sent his friend to get Omega ready to move out. He stood across the street from the staging area, thinking of his soldiers within. Did they doubt? Would they follow him for the rest of the mission?

Would they leave him to walk alone into the center of Hell—or rather, into whatever horrible Circle he would be trapped in for eternity? Ramirez shook his head.

Virgil walked out of the Staging Area and across the quiet street toward Ramirez. His face was blank and impossible to read.

"Your men have pushed forward admirably, soldier," Virgil said. He stood with his hands folded inside the wide sleeves of his cloak. "Are you sure you want to press forward?"

"It's not a matter of wanting or not wanting. Our mission is to go to the center. We're trained for this—"

"Oh, I know. Supernatural forces leave their mark on the soul. I can read the magic remnants on your being as easily as if they were written on your face. Do you know the difference between the witch doctors and sorcerers and psychics you've fought and the predicament you currently find yourself in? Eventually those poor bastards wind up *here*."

"This is what we do," Ramirez continued. "We were trained for this, or something like it… If we give up and stay here then hope really is lost."

"Did you not read the signs on the Doorway?" Virgil cracked a smile. "Abandon *all* hope."

Any other day, any other time, the Lieutenant would've laughed.

Ramirez sighed. "Should we just stay here? An eternity in a prison must be better than an eternity of torture."

Virgil glanced back with disdain at Staging Area Bravo and the soldiers within. "They are all biding their time. They will all fall. They cannot go back because they are afraid, and it is only a matter of time before they push forward.

"I do not trivialize your mission. To push forward is the more damning choice."

Ramirez paused, not to consider any choices of what to do, but to think of anything he could ask the guide while he was talkative.

"Padre, guíanos… How on Earth did anyone even make it this far? He thought of the Hallway, the Pit, the Field, and the Parlor and how many men must have been lost to the creatures within.

"It is not the skill of the soldier, but the weight of the sin that determines who passes through a Circle and who comes to rest within."

Ramirez's eyes widened in realization. The Lieutenant knew his soldiers. He thought of the men he lost in each Circle: Turner, Harris, and Lee were womanizers and had been taken in the Hallway—the Circle of Lust. Young was an unknown and taken in the Circle of Gluttony. Smith was a gambler and taken in the Circle of Greed. Miller… Well, Miller was an asshole as prone to outbursts. He'd been taken in Wrath.

Virgil continued, "Some of your soldiers might have passed through the lower circles unscathed, but if there are darker sins in them then they will not make it through. The inner circles are vicious and unforgiving. They are reserved for the worst offenses and punished accordingly."

"…How can I know who will make it?"

"You cannot. It is between each man and God."

"I don't suppose you can give me a heads up on what Circles are next, can you?"

Virgil shook his head. "Rules."

Ramirez stared blankly across the city. He tried not to think because he felt that if he *started* thinking then his head would spin.

He chuckled instead. Virgil looked at him quizzically.

The one thought that had popped into Ramirez's head, was about how they lost more men to Lust than Wrath.

~

Dr. David Levy

David laid on the bare concrete floor of Staging Area Bravo across the room from Nancy. She was sitting next to the soldier, Kim, who was crying quietly against her shoulder. He hadn't spoken much, so Nancy hadn't either.

The soldiers of Omega Squad were interspersed with those of Bravo—not to talk, but because they had simply laid down wherever there was an open spot. Some of the soldiers started praying. One of the Omega soldiers left the circle and came over. He slumped down next to David and introduced himself as Clark.

He nodded while he talked and kept his eyes on the prayer circle. "Didn't much care for it, myself," he said quietly. David assumed he was talking about their praying. "*I know* for a fact some of those men don't either. Nothing like putting on a show when you're already in Hell."

"Can you blame them?" David asked.

"I didn't say that. I just don't want to have any part of it."

"I considered it," David said, surprising himself. "I considered believing. Repenting."

"It would be the smart thing to do. Jump out of the way of the car before it hits you. So why don't you?"

"Because there's probably a worse place for people who pretend to believe." Both men chuckled at the black humor.

"I knew you were one of them," Clark added. "An atheist, I mean."

David grunted as he rolled over onto his back. It was both a question to the statement and a protest about the floor.

Clark went on, "I have a sixth sense sometimes about other atheists."

"Only sometimes?"

He continued flatly, "It's like gaydar, but for those who don't believe in God." Clark got up and added that he was going to take a walk.

"That's it?" David asked. "As soon as I think I might get to converse with a Special Forces soldier, they get up and leave?"

Clark nodded.

"You just wanted to make sure your atheist-dar still worked?"

Clark nodded again. "I would've stayed longer if it didn't." David looked at him with a question. The soldier continued, "I'm not trying to hang out too long next to you. We're both going to get taken in the same Circle."

David had managed to doze off here and there but sleep was fleeting when you had to roll every few minutes on a hard surface. Between that and where they were and talking with Clark, the translator was surprised he got any sleep at all. It was like trying to sleep during a severe thunderstorm or the night before vacation. A stomach churning mix of excitement and dread, except that he felt ridiculous trying to describe it. How could his brain possibly equate any of those things to what he was feeling now?

Footsteps echoed from outside. The Lieutenant and the Sergeant were back and both stood tall at the edge of the room.

"On your feet, Omega. Ready in five," the Lieutenant ordered.

David's heart sank—felt as if it dropped somewhere into the floor. So that was it? Their short respite was over. It was off to the next Circle. To the next roll of the dice.

David looked around from the floor and realized that no one had moved. A room full of soldiers looked at the Lieutenant with the same blank stare. The air grew tense and heavy with all that was unspoken in that order. *On your feet. Ready in five. Go to the next Circle. Somewhere we'll all die.*

The Sergeant stepped forward. "On your feet, Omega. Now!"

Omega Squad did stand up, but in spite of the Sergeant's tone, they got up slowly. Across from David, Nancy stirred and pushed herself up. David did the same—it felt automatic, like he was being swept away with the tide rather than his body moving because he willed it.

They soldiers and the translators gathered at the door and the Lieutenant led them through a prayer. "I am an Omega Soldier. I will bravely go to places that don't exist and against beings that strike fear into the hearts of men. I am a beacon in the darkness and a bastion against the occult. My will is incorruptible and my body is my own. *Mi voluntad es incorruptible y mi cuerpo es mío.*"

Nancy mumbled the words to herself, but David couldn't bring himself to bow his head or to repeat them. Neither could most of the soldiers.

~ ~ ~

The Kiln

Dr. David Levy

Virgil led the soldiers through the empty city of Dis and to the next Circle of Hell. This would be the sixth Circle and though they had not measured the circles as they passed through, David felt that the Circles were getting narrower. It felt like they passed through the city of Dis in a fraction of the time of the other circles.

But then maybe that was because the city was empty and no torture was going on there.

The guide led them through several connected buildings, all the same bare concrete. The only thing that gave the sense of progress was the changing architecture: One building was open and filled with stairways, another was curved with arched halls, and the final was dark and square, and reminded David fiercely of the Parlor.

He started to sweat, at first thinking it was from his growing fear, but then one of the soldiers behind him complained about the heat.

From up ahead Virgil said plainly, "We have passed into the sixth Circle: The Kiln."

It was getting dark now, nearly enough for their red flashlights, but Omega kept them off. The Kiln was rows and rows of passageways, like the Hallway, except that Omega Squad was completely alone. Somewhere in the next several steps, David was aware of muted sounds echoing from down the hall… or maybe coming from the walls around them. As they walked deeper into the Kiln it grew steadily, but it sounded like it might have been static or wind or…

The sounds grew and grew until it was clear what they were: They were muffled screams from somewhere in the walls, so distorted they sounded like wind.

Virgil paused for a moment at an intersection, as if to get his bearings.

David stared at the wall next to him. Somewhere along the twists and turns of the Kiln, the surface had changed. They were no longer smooth concrete, but rose and fell like waves. At the crest of each wave was a slit that went from the floor almost all the way to the ceiling. Now that they were stopped, David realized that one muffled scream was coming directly from that wave.

Written on the stone was: *η ψυχή δεν πεθαίνει με το σώμα.* *The soul does not die with the body.*

Against his better judgement, David reached out and felt the stone. It was hot to the touch and the stone vibrated faintly. He could *feel* the screams.

People were in the walls—trapped in the stone.

The feeling of dread that overcame him was unlike anything he had felt in life or since he'd walked through the doors of

Hell. It was sudden and complete, like a lightswitch had been flipped somewhere in his soul. Hope went dark.

Virgil and the Lieutenant talked somewhere up ahead. Their voices were distant and muffled, much like the ones trapped in the walls. In the near-darkness, it was impossible to tell how far away they were. David tried to call out to them, but his throat was parched and his voice raspy. The rest of the squad felt impossibly far away.

David grabbed desperately and he latched onto the arm of the soldier closest to him.

He looked at the translator questioningly, completely oblivious to the crisis David was having. "Dr. Levy, keep it together, man," the soldier said. His voice was normal, clear.

It was enough. David was still with soldiers. Still with Nancy. Nancy was one soldier behind him. Virgil and the Lieutenant were just up ahead.

Hope was dim.

They marched on. The temperature of the Kiln rose and rose the further they walked. David had sweat through his fatigues. The air was warm and dry, and it was getting hard to breath. His breathing drowned out the screams from the walls and the footsteps of Omega in the dim halls.

Above the passageway: *Nullius desperandum est, ut sciatur vir passus in aeternum cumque putarunt brevis in interitum eius.*

No man has known despair, such as the man suffering in eternity when he thought his afterlife short.

"Are you okay, David?" Nancy asked from behind him. She had pushed past the soldier between them and clutched his arm.

"I think so," he lied.

"You're sweating like a pig."

"I'll be better once we're through this blasted place."

Nancy held David's hand; she felt cool by comparison. She wasn't sweating.

"I'm sure it's just a little bit further," she said, offering what little comfort she could in those tortured depths.

David smiled at her and whispered, "Thanks. Are you feeling okay?"

"As well as can be expected."

But as soon as her voice left, the hallway felt empty again. He glanced back at the squad, but no one met his eyes—no one except Clark. The atheist stared at him, wide-eyed, face frozen in surprise. The sound of footsteps was gone and David's own labored breathing filled his ears. He glanced at the person-sized waves in the walls and his mind flashed to images of people trapped within, completely alone in the dark and the heat.

Virgil's voice. "Those trapped inside the stone thought they knew all of the world from what they could see, hear, and observe. They claimed the soul died with the body. Their false prophecies have made them right. Now they shall spend an eternity knowing nothing but hellfire. Unable to see, hear or know anything outside of their suffering."

Again David felt that feeling of dread, of someone reaching for the lightswitch to completely turn off all hope.

Panicked breathing now. Virgil was still talking, but his voice was muffled and impossibly far away. Omega Squad was somewhere in the dim. Nancy's hand was gone.

David reached out, desperate to find her or the nearby soldiers—desperate to find anyone—but felt only stone. Stone all around. At some point the light had gone out—the switch was flipped. David couldn't even see his own hands.

The air was heavy with dread. It loomed around him like a mist.

Hope was gone and in those terrified moments, David wondered if he could remember it at all. Had it abandoned him or had he abandoned it when he passed through the Doorway?

Nancy's voice on the other side of the stone, muffled and faint. "David, oh Jesus! David!"

"Nancy!"

David had hoped it was a trick. Just another trick… but then Nancy flipped the switch—

"Oh God! He's on the other side of the wall."

David's strength went out like the tide. He would've collapsed to his knees if it weren't for the warm concrete tomb wrapped around him.

"David, we're going to get you out…" Nancy kept talking to him through the walls, but her voice receded like his strength and was replaced by his own desperate breathing. The air in his tomb grew warm and then hot.

"Please don't leave me," David called out. "Please—don't—leave me." It hurt to talk and then it hurt to breathe. The air was hot and dry. His calls turned to whispers and coughs.

The stone wrapping his body burned and he desperately tried to pull away from it, but when he did David only pressed himself harder against the other side.

Somewhere in the pain, hope was forgotten. The world was replaced with the roar of fire.

His coughs turned to screams.

~

Lieutenant Hector Ramirez

Dr. Reed was holding onto one of Kim and sobbing quietly, her sadness blending in with the muted screams of agony from within the stone. It was like a terrible symphony. Kim's rifle hung at his side and he held the horrified translator, running a hand over her hair.

No one had seen Dr. Levy disappear. One second he was there, the next he was gone. Somehow Dr. Reed had found him in the wall and talked to him during his final moments, until his voice became nothing but another muffled scream.

Clark was gone too. He had suffered the same fate as Dr. Levy. Another victim of the Circle. In the panic of the moment, the men noticed now and called out for him. Their shouts echoed down the hall and were drowned out by the static of screams.

There was a small flame of anger burning in Ramirez, but it was smothered by dread. There were six of them left now: Davis, Gomez, Dr. Reed, Sergeant Wilson and himself… Was that how it was going to be? Would they lose a soldier to every Circle? The slow inevitable downfall of Omega, and Ramirez was walking his soldiers right through it.

They could fight the supernatural. They had fought dozens of such threats on every continent. But they couldn't fight this. Each Circle of Hell had taken soldiers before Omega could fight back or even assess…

But there was no assessing to be done, was there? It wasn't the creatures of the Circles that were picking off his men one-by-one. Virgil said each of the soldiers would succumb to whatever sin—whatever fate—they had succumbed to in life.

Their final resting places within the Circles were already determined.

They couldn't fight fate.

Lieutenant Ramirez ordered them onward. One of the soldiers grunted in frustration. Maybe Gomez. Dr. Reed's sobs turned into sniffles. Ramirez understood—he wasn't a machine—but they had a mission to complete. There was no chiseling Dr. Levy or Clark out of the walls just as there was no saving Smith or Miller or any of the other soldiers they had lost.

They each had their own fate.

If Ramirez could last long enough, maybe he could give the fallen angel at the center a piece of his mind.

~

The Lake

Lieutenant Hector Ramirez

Omega Squad pushed through the final corridors of the Kiln. They turned one last corner and saw the exit. Dark tunnels and muffled screams gave way to overwhelming red right and roaring wind. Sand littered the hallway. The Lieutenant gripped his rifle tighter as they walked the last steps.

When they reached the end and his eyes adjusted he saw a massive red lake—an ocean. Its waters stretched out to the horizon in every direction except for the one they came from. The dark red waters churned and frothed. Where waves should've made whitecaps, instead bursts of flames erupted into the sky. Steam rose off of the surface. The heat made gusts of wind that blew violently and carried up the smell of burning flesh. Ramirez felt like he was looking at the surface of the sun.

The hallway exited out of the cave wall and onto a sandy beach. Yellow-orange—the color of fire. The packed sand sloped gently down to the water while the wind roared around them—but much like the Kiln, the sound here wasn't truly wind.

Down in the water, hands and mouths thrashed, struggling to stay above the water or to get out of the water. Flames licked those pitiful souls that managed to break the surface. The roaring wind was a mix of steam and the frothing screams of millions of souls burning alive.

Up above, the cave walls rose up to a ceiling miles above the surface, hidden by swirling white and black smoke. Pinpricks of light dotted the sky, appearing and disappearing like tiny lightning bolts. They dotted the sky as far as Ramirez could see. Dots of lightning flashed close near them and seconds later people dropped out of the sky, plummeting into the churning ocean of fire.

Virgil turned to Omega and to Dr. Reed. "This is the Lake of Violence and the Seventh Circle. We must go in. Beneath the surface. Your mission lies down there." Their guide took three steps into the boiling waters.

Lieutenant Ramirez walked forward and stopped shin-deep in the blood red waters—but no fire burned him and he didn't so much as flinch. The water didn't even look like it was steaming near him.

Sergeant Wilson called to Virgil over the roaring winds, "You're already dead. How do we know that it won't hurt us?"

Virgil shrugged. "You have had faith in me thus far."

Lieutenant Ramirez lowered his rifle and walked up to the Lake. In spite of the steam and heat, he knelt down next to the edge and pulled off a glove. Slowly, reached a hand toward the waters. The heat built, but when he touched the water, it felt lukewarm to the touch. He paused in disbelief before reaching his entire hand in. No pain, not even discomfort. Ramirez pulled his hand away and looked it over. His skin looked completely fine—it wasn't even wet.

He turned, overcome with a small sense of wonder, and called out, "We're going swimming, boys."

To his surprise, Dr. Nancy Reed was the first one to walk forward. She reached the edge and dipped a foot in before stepping in shin-deep. Sergeant Wilson walked in next. Kim walked up next and into the water, sharing Ramirez's surprise.

"Come on, soldiers," he called back to Davis and Gomez.

Both soldiers walked up but stopped three yards short. Davis tried inching forward, but backed away. "It's too hot," he said, covering his face like he was close to an open flame. "How are you guys standing in that? It's like a bonfire. What kind of voodoo bullshit is this!"

Ramirez turned to Virgil and grabbed him by the collar of his cloak. "What's going on?" he demanded.

Virgil shrugged. "A mortal in Hell knows no danger, unless he passes through his destined Circle. Only those prone to violence feel the fires of the Lake. That is why they cannot pass without suffering."

Lieutenant Ramirez turned back to the two soldiers.

"What should we do, sir?" Gomez asked.

Before Ramirez could answer, the ground between them shuddered. Sand shifted and rolled down the slope. Then hands reached out of the ground, thin with jagged fingers and clawed for Davis and Gomez. The two soldiers shouldered their rifles and shuffled backward, toward the entrance to the Kiln. The smell of sulfur blew across the beach.

More hands reached for them, surrounded them and sliced gashes in their pant-legs. They opened fire on the creatures in the ground. Gunfire drowned out the roar of the wind. Lieu-tenant Ramirez, Sergeant Wilson, and Kim shouldered their rifles and shot at the ground in front of the soldiers, trying to cover their retreat.

Heads and shoulders rose up out of the sand—twisted crea-tures like the imps of the Parlor. Their skin was spackled with red clumps of sand. They gnashed jagged teeth at the two sol-diers on the bank of the Lake.

Bullets tore through the creatures, bullets laced with silver and stamped with runes, and creatures cried out—their gut-tural language somewhere between smashed bricks and ringing bells. A cacophony of screams and gunshots echoed through the cave and over the hellfire waters.

Creatures exploded as bullets tore through them. Sulfur drenched the air and Ramirez wretched so hard he stopped firing. Dr. Reed fell hands and knees into the water as she coughed. Davis and Gomez screamed curses as they shuffled back to the Kiln's entrance. They were back to back now, one shooting creatures in their path and the other shooting at crea-tures that leapt at them from behind.

Sergeant Wilson and Kim started to run toward the soldiers, but creatures turned and screamed at them, blocking the way. Even as they opened fire and tore through several, the crea-tures didn't attack. They merely kept Wilson and Kim from approaching the other soldiers.

Davis and Gomez were nearly at the entrance to the Kiln.

Spit and bile dribbled from Ramirez's mouth as his cough-ing fit subsided. Just in time to realize with horror that the entire wall of the cave, as high up as he could see, was writhing. Creatures were coming from above now. They sprung free from the wall and fell down toward the unsuspecting soldiers, building like an avalanche until they blotted out the cave around them. Davis and Gomez looked like toy soldiers in comparison.

Ramirez, Wilson, Kim and Dr. Reed watched from the shore in open-mouthed horror as the living avalanche crashed on two of the last soldiers of Omega. Gunfire stopped and for a moment the only sounds were the horrid screams of the creatures. Some bounced off the sand and into the lake of fire. The rest swarmed aimlessly on the shore in a pile two stories high.

Then Davis and Gomez were dragged to the top of the pile, so small against the mass that they were only visible because of their black uniforms. They flailed as the creatures passed them like a conveyor belt toward the Lake. The mass of creatures flowed down into the Lake as they carried the soldiers, the creatures in the fire screamed out as they were burned alive, sacrificing themselves for the fate of the damned.

On the shore, Sergeant Wilson and Kim shouldered their rifles and screamed as they fired into the mass. Ramirez could only watch. Davis and Gomez reached the peninsula of the mass of creatures and tumbled over the edge into the Lake. Their screams drowned out by the cacophony of infernal noises and gunfire. The soldiers of Omega Squad plunged into the blood red waters.

When the task was done the creatures climbed over one another, leaving their dying brethren in the waters. Back on shore, they climbed back into the sand and back up the walls of the cave, as if each creature was going back to its own hole.

The remnants of Omega watched in muted horror as the last of the creatures burrowed into the sand and into the rock of the cave walls. When they had all disappeared there weren't even footsteps left in the sand to mark their fate.

All that was left of their squad was the Lieutenant, the Sergeant, Kim, and Dr. Nancy Reed.

Lieutenant Ramirez said his grandfather's prayer quietly, "*Padre, dame tu fuerza, tu misericordia y tu sabiduría.*" Father, lend me your strength, your mercy, and your wisdom.

Virgil waited, expectantly. Knee-deep in the blood water of the Lake.

"Fuck you," Sergeant Wilson called to their guide. "I'm not going any further."

"Yes you are, soldier," the Lieutenant replied without looking at him.

"What's the point?"

"The mission is to go to the center." Ramirez turned to his second-in-command, to his friend. Kim and Dr. Reed stood beside the Lieutenant, heads bowed, not offering support to one side or the other.

Wilson shrugged, a sarcastic smile on his face. "The squad is gone. We're not mission capable anymore."

"What are you going to do, go back?" Ramirez chuckled. "Think about all the soldiers we passed at the Staging Areas. Don't you think those soldiers would've gone back if they could?" The Lieutenant turned to Virgil. "We can't go back, can we?"

Virgil answered reluctantly. "You would be treated like your two soldiers just now. The demons won't let you leave. You're here, just as surely as you would be if you died. If you belong here, then here you will stay."

Ramirez looked to his friend, but Wilson wasn't swayed. "I don't know if you've noticed this, Atticus, but these things don't just attack us."

"Unless you belong there. How many Circles are left?"

"Two more after the Lake," Virgil answered. Behind him, souls of the damned fell in a steady drizzle into the flaming waters, their splashes indistinguishable from the millions drowning on the surface.

"Fuck those odds, *sir.* I'll take my chances." Sergeant Wilson half turned, as if he was hesitant to go. As if there was something he wanted to say or was waiting for the Lieutenant to say.

But Ramirez could only think of the betrayal of his friend leaving him so deep in Hell. Anger boiled in him, overshadowing the fire of the Lake.

"What do you even have back there, huh?" Ramirez sneered. "You've given up on life back home—"

"Don't you think I wanted *something* back home? Just because I wasn't any good at it doesn't mean I didn't want my own life eventually. I'm not going to live this forever, Hector. Are you? Don't you even want to get home to Tracey?"

"Of course I do," Ramirez said automatically. He took a deep breath. "I'm sorry. We just… We need to focus on the mission. You're still in Omega. We're in this together."

"We're going to die in here," Wilson said, the fight going out of his voice.

"You're a good man, Atticus—

"And the others weren't?"

Ramirez didn't have an answer for that. He thought all his soldiers were good, decent men. Sure, they had faults, but who didn't? *Let he who is without sin cast the first stone.*

Where they all damned to stay down here? Ramirez looked out over the lake of fire and the souls falling from the cave and down into its waters.

What was his sin?

Before Ramirez could dwell too long on his question, Kim said, "There's probably a Circle down here for abandoning missions."

Ramirez, Wilson, and Nancy all chuckled. It was weak and pitiful against the overwhelming horror of the scene, but it was just enough. Kim smiled.

Sergeant Wilson looked around the cave and the lake, his eyes glistening. "I'm scared."

Ramirez had never heard the words from his friend before and he had never seen him so shaken. Instead of trying to bolster Atticus and remind him that he was a good man, Ramirez simply said, "Me too."

It was enough. Sergeant Wilson nodded, wiped his eyes, and walked down the beach to join the remnants of his squad.

Virgil walked deeper into the lake and instead of swimming across the surface, he merely walked until his head disappeared beneath the surface.

The Lieutenant, the Sergeant, Kim, and Dr. Reed shared a look and then followed him. The water was lukewarm as it rose against Ramirez's stomach and chest, and then he held his breath and submerged his head completely under. Inadvertently he closed his eyes.

It didn't feel like he was in water at all.

Ramirez opened his eyes. Instead of nearly opaque water, the world around him was a warm haze of blood-red mist, like a morning in a jungle. The Lake's surface was an undulating ceiling above him that sparkled with flame. In the distance, poor souls dropped into the surface and drowned in fire.

Virgil walked steadily in front of them, not giving them a moment to pause or think. All four jogged to catch up to their guide. Their bodies and limbs moved like they were up on dry-land instead of under the water.

Down here, the roar of the wind and fire, and the howl of screams were gone—the air was completely still and silent except for their quiet footsteps on the sand.

They followed the slope down and down. The sand of the Lakebed splayed out before them like the side of a mountain too massive to fathom. As far as they could see, damned souls hung in the red. No matter how they flailed, they hung impotently in the water.

As they descended, the mist and the red glow of the Lake faded. Deeper and deeper into the Lake, until the air was dry and clear. The red waters of the lake were nothing but sky above them.

A forest rose in the distance.

"Virgil, what were those things back there?" Ramirez asked. "I smelled sulfur. They weren't people, were they?"

"They are demons, the caretakers of Hell. They oversee the tortures of the Hallway, the Parlor and the Lake—though they roam *all* Circles, just behind the veil of reality."

"Jesus," Kim said. "You mean those people in the Hall-way… Those were demons?"

The image of Not-Tracey flashed in Ramirez's mind. He had known it wasn't her. He shuddered. That *thing* had been a demon.

A few steps later, Virgil added, "They used to be angels. They are the pitiful remnants of the weakest angels that fell from Heaven. Now they are so twisted they don't remember where they came from."

Somehow that was a small thing compared to the image of Not-Tracey, which was seared in the Lieutenant's mind.

They passed from desert into a sparse forest filled with tall, gnarled trees. The bark was splintered and grotesque, with sore-like growths of black, weeping sap. Their roots twisted up through the sand and tangled the spaces between the trees like overgrown brush.

When they got close to the treeline, their group slowed. The branches high above were completely bare. No leaves were on the branches—but bodies hung from the trees.

A single noose hung from each tree and a single body hung by the neck from each noose.

"Oh shit," Kim said from the back of the group. He mumbled incoherently while looking up at the grisly canopy.

"Is this the eighth Circle?" the Sergeant asked.

"No," Virgil replied. "The Lake of Violence has three sections. The fiery surface is for tyrants and murderers and those who took pleasure in violent acts. We are passing into the second section, the Brake. It is home to those who committed violence against their own bodies. *Suicides.*"

There were faces in the trees—not carved or drawn, but made from the bark itself. The faces of the dead above were the same as those in the trees. As Ramirez and Omega pushed onward, stepping carefully through the roots of those first trees, they heard quick creaks and groans of wood around them. The trees didn't move, but their beady eyes followed Ramirez and the others through the woods.

Virgil continued, "They are fated to do nothing but watch as the Circle continues on around them, deprived of the bodies they took from themselves."

"What's wrong?" Nancy whispered from behind them.

Ramirez turned to see her consoling Kim. He was doubled over, shuffling his steps.

"This is it," he mumbled. Thick spit dribbled from his mouth. "I'm not going to make it."

"Nonsense," Nancy said, rubbing his shoulders. "I'm sure we're almost through. Just a little further, right Virgil?"

Their stoic guide looked off into the woods. "*We* have miles to go."

Kim groaned in pain and when he looked up, Ramirez finally saw why. His skin was darkening, stiffening and now had deep cracks in it that ooze black. The same black sap hung in strands from his mouth. He tried to walk, but the same creaks and groans that came from the trees sounded from Kim's legs as he shuffled.

He finally shook his head and stopped in a small clearing in the Brake. Even though he stopped, his body still changed. His shoulders and legs grew, splitting his fatigues. His cheeks and forehead split and oozed sap. Within a minute he was seven feet tall. Kim breathed quickly, as if it hurt to breathe deeper. His face winced with the little expression he had left.

"I was seventeen," Kim said. He shook his head as if he didn't want to remember. "I hoped... I hoped that living would be enough to forget—enough to be forgiven. It feels like a lifetime ago, but I can still remember how it felt that night… Doesn't matter how long ago it felt. There's no outrunning the past." He called to Virgil, eyes shut, "Did I—did I ever have a chance?"

Virgil turned, his own eyes glistening. "Perhaps, but it is not in my wisdom to say. Just as it was not I who made the rules nor I who slit your wrists." The guide looked away quickly.

"I can't move," Kim said. He shuddered and his body groaned so loud it echoed through the forest. "It's fucked up that I'm the last one left." He winced a smile.

"No, you're not," Ramirez said as he looked Kim in the eyes. "Omega is right here with you. We're right here with you."

Kim met his eyes and Ramirez imagined he said thanks.

The soldier's fatigues split completely as his body erupted in a mountain of bark. The horrid creaking of wood was deafening as Kim was transformed in an instant into another one of the trees of the Brake. The Lieutenant, the Sergeant and Dr. Reed were sent sprawling back.

Ramirez had fallen to the ground. When he looked up from his back, he saw Kim's body hanging from the top of the tree, wearing new fatigues. The face in the tree—his face—stared at them, unblinking.

The Lieutenant tried to mutter his grandfather's prayer, but the words came out breathlessly. He tried to sit up, but he only managed to get to his knees. He stared back at the bark-frozen soldier and felt the weight of the mission.

"I'm sorry," Ramirez muttered. He couldn't bring himself to look at what remained of Kim. Could he have turned back?

Could he have at least spared some of his men from their fates? Even if… Even if they still wound up in Hell, at least that way they would've lived a little longer.

The weight of the loss of each of his men came crashing down on him. The sky felt like it had dropped on him and Ramirez felt in that moment like he might retch up his soul.

"God, what have I done?" Hector Ramirez sobbed quietly in despair.

When the world felt the smallest and his guilt was an infinite black pit opening up beneath his feet, he felt the arms of Atticus and Nancy around his shoulders. Reminding him that he wasn't alone. Somehow that made Hector cry even harder.

Ramirez walked, or rather his body walked. He felt hollow. His body was moving without input. He saw things, but his brain didn't process. He heard things but everything seemed impossibly far aware. Like he was living a dream.

The mangled trees of the Brake gave way to a barren dunes. The sand was warm beneath their feet and the breeze was steady across the sand. Above, the sky was a distant swirling red—from that far away it was incomprehensible to Ramirez that same red was the Lake of fire.

Fire rained from the sky in a steady downpour, leaving clumps of burning sand, which smoldered and added to the dunes beneath their feet.

They passed lonely souls burning alive. The same sand that Ramirez, Wilson, Dr. Reed, and Virgil walked on without care, scorched the skin of everyone else. Each person rolled on the ground in agony as fire burst up from the sand wherever they touched it. The constant rain of fire did the same, leaving burning welts wherever they fell. Their skin was charred and black from the constant assault. They were in so much pain that they didn't notice the four pilgrims passing by.

Virgil narrated as they walked, "Those that have perverted the creations of God—nature and art—are destined to spend their days the burning, barren plane of the Desert; a place devoid of both beautiful things. They cannot even draw in the sand because of the pain."

Ramirez saw all these things. He heard the screams carried across the dunes. He smelled the burning flesh. But he didn't feel any of it.

~ ~ ~

The Chasm and
the Steps

Lieutenant Hector Ramirez

In the distance there was nothing and the sight made them pause.

The barren dunes of the Desert gave way to the Chasm. Sand turned to stone under their feet as they walked to the precipice. They neared the edge and the wind stopped. It felt like the world was completely still. The sky above was clear and a faint pink—they were so far below the lake of violence that it was little more than a smudge in the clouds.

In front of them there was nothing but black as the Chasm stretched out past the horizon and seemed to swallow all light.

But to the sides, the Chasm curved. For the first time they could see the curve of a Circle of Hell. They were growing smaller as Omega Squad got closer to the center.

The Chasm was unfathomable but it wasn't infinite.

Ramirez peered over the edge. Miles below, the Chasm was lined with rings—with terraces—on which a cliffside city was built. On the curve of the cliffs, Ramirez counted twelve distinct terrace levels, each dropping hundreds of feet to the level below. Beyond that, the Chasm dropped into darkness. His heart raced with vertigo.

"Where the Hell do we go now?" Sergeant Wilson asked.

Calmly, Virgil answered, "We must go down. To the center."

Before the Sergeant could ask *how* they were supposed to get down the sheer walls a swirling black form appeared in the darkness below. A curling, scaled serpent rose from the depths. The creature rose at alarming speed, growing massive as it passed the terraces, carried by gargoyle wings bigger than any plane Ramirez had ever seen.

Lieutenant Ramirez and Sergeant Wilson shouldered their rifles and backed away with Dr. Reed from the edge. Virgil stared down at the approaching creature.

Ramirez called to him but their guide didn't budge, even as wind blasted up the side of the cliff and the creature slammed into the cliffside. The ground continued to shake as the creature clawed itself the rest of the way up the wall. Ramirez and the others were nearly bowled over by the quake.

Virgil didn't even flinch when the massive head crested the edge and rose even further, exploding upwards from behind the cliff. The monster's neck curved so that it was looking down on them from two stories up while its shoulders were hidden below the edge. It had the boxy snout of a lion, but it was covered with scales. Ramirez struggled to keep the whole of it in focus—the dragon's head and neck were thicker than a semi-truck and ripple with coils of muscle as if snakes lived under its skin.

The dragon regarded them with narrow vertical pupils.

Virgil turned. "The monster, Geryon, will accompany us through the Steps of Fraud. There are other ways down, but he is magnitudes quicker than any others."

"I—I don't know," Dr. Reed said. She was backing away from the dragon.

"You have nothing to fear from him," Virgil offered. "He will carry us in his claws past the ten levels of the Steps. Trust me, you do not want to pass through the city of Malbolge that lines the cliff."

She shook her head, mouth open in silent horror. "It's not too late," she whispered. "We could go back. There's nothing in the center for us."

Instead of Virgil, Geryon spoke. His mouth opened and Ramirez winced in expectation of a booming voice, but Geryon's voice was quiet—human-like—and smooth. It was the voice of a narrator, not a dragon.

"You must come with me. If you go back, you will not survive the Lake of Violence. Only Virgil has safe passage from the denizens of Hell."

Dr. Reed seemed even more scared after hearing Geryon speak. "Are you a prisoner in this Circle too, Geryon?"

"Yes."

"Then you are a liar. I won't go with you." She turned to Lieutenant Ramirez and Sergeant Wilson. "There's nothing left for me. Nothing to translate. There weren't any words in the Lake and there won't be any words worth translating past here." Finally she pleaded with them, "Please. Don't do this. Don't go."

"We're going," Lieutenant Ramirez said, cutting off his friend. "Last chance, Dr. Reed."

She shook her head violently. "I won't go."

Ramirez nodded. "We'll come back for you." Then he looked at his friend. Atticus Wilson nodded in reply. "We're ready," Ramirez said to the dragon.

"Very well." Geryon crawled up the cliffside, revealing half a dozen clawed hands. As each hand appeared, they grabbed a traveler one by one; Virgil, the Lieutenant, and the Sergeant. The Dragon's grip was cold and firm, and pinned Ramirez's hands to his side. Its great wings flapped three times before it turned and flew away and left Dr. Reed in wide-mouthed horror on the edge of the Chasm. Geryon rose in the air and flew out across the Steps before descending.

When Dr. Reed was just a dot on the cliff, Ramirez heard the entire cliffside rumble and then watched in shock as a section of rocks gave way. The dot plummeted with the rubble.

In another set of Geryon's claws, Sergeant Wilson was screaming for them to go back for her.

"She would have fallen either way," Geryon said, "by my grip or by the rocks. Do not worry. She will survive the fall. Survive and live out her sentence in the city of Malbolge."

Sergeant Wilson screamed in frustration, but Ramirez couldn't see his friend from the way Geryon's claws were turned.

"She committed fraud?" Ramirez asked, still staring at the marred cliffside. He wondered what it might have been? Then he remembered the research papers that scientists are expected to publish.

"She must have," Virgil said from another claw. "There are no accidents in Hell."

Ramirez wondered what exactly she had faked in her papers. Was it just a detail—no, somehow that didn't seem like it would be enough. Had she faked the whole paper? Maybe even the paper that made her famous—famous enough to be one of the top names in her field. One of the first people the brass would call for a mission like this.

Geryon descended with Ramirez, Wilson, and Virgil down into the Chasm. It clutched clawed hands close across its chest, bringing the remnants of Omega close enough to talk as they flew. The Lieutenant stared, wide-eyed at the city of Malbolge spread across the terrace layers of the Chasm. Malbolge really was a city in every sense of the word: Every inch was packed with carved stone buildings and people.

Somehow there seemed like there were even more souls here than in the Pit full of piles of writhing people.

"How are there so many people?" he asked.

"The Steps of Fraud are many times smaller than the outer rings, as one would expect," Virgil replied, "but there didn't used to be quite so many souls packed within its limits. In your time, the sowers of Fraud have grown by magnitudes even the denizens of Hell could not have foreseen. You see, when man's voice was physical he could only deceive his neighbors. In the era of written word, maybe deceive a few more if he could write. In the digital age, everyone has the voice of a king. Lies spread as easily as the wind and not enough people care to tell the difference."

Ramirez looked down from Geryon's claws at the incomprehensibleness of Malbolge. How many of the people he knew would wind up there or in some other corner of Hell? How many faces would he recognize? The thought of seeing a loved one down there terrified him more than any other horror he had seen.

Beside him, Virgil narrated the Steps of Fraud. Lieutenant Ramirez half-listened, hollow with grief.

The guide spoke of each Step, the fraudulent souls contained within, and the punishments they endured. They descended in low, circling swoops, as if Geryon was humoring Virgil's narration. Among those named were Panderers, Seducers, Flatterers, Astrologists, Bribers, Hypocrites, Thieves, False Prophets and False Spiritual Counselors, Sowers of Discord. There were ten Steps in all, though Ramirez knew he'd missed much of Virgil's explanation.

"A whole city of liars," Ramirez said absently.

The guide added, "Imagine every possible relationship, no matter whether it was casual, service, media, familial, intimate, social, or sexual—nothing is true. Everyone you meet is a deceiver, including your own face in the mirror. Imagine that and you still cannot fathom the city of Fraud."

As Geryon spiraled down and down, Ramirez felt despair fill the hollow space inside him.

Sergeant Wilson called up to them. "Are there any other creatures like you here?"

Virgil answered for the dragon. "You mean others such as Geryon, or Charon the boatman? Yes, there are a great many strange and wondrous damned things imprisoned here. Remember that you have only seen a small sliver of Hell. Within its walls lie creatures mythical, biblical and those from times before man had words. Some of them even lord over their own slivers of Hell, masters of their pitiful domains."

The dragon stopped somewhere below the tenth step of Fraud and set the two soldiers and one guide down on an outcropping of rock maybe ten feet across. Below them, impossibly far down, the darkness glowed blue-black.

Virgil pointed to a crevice just barely big enough for a man. "There is our passage down. The Well is all that remains."

Ramirez followed Virgil down into the darkness of the crevice and toward whatever fate awaited them. Sergeant Wilson was just behind him. Even between the three men in the dark of the passage, close enough to hear them, Ramirez felt completely alone in his despair.

Geryon waited until the three were safely inside the crevice before departing, shaking the Chasm.

~ ~ ~

The Well

Lieutenant Hector Ramirez

Climbing down through the crevice was an isolating, nervous task. He couldn't really twist his body and headlamp to look down, so he had to lower a boot down and feel for each foothold blindly. Somehow he managed not to step on Virgil below him.

The air temperature plummeted and the frost of Ramirez's breath obscured his head lamp. The rocks of the cave were equally cold and as Lieutenant Ramirez, Sergeant Wilson and their guide descended, the rocks grew slick with ice. Their military boots and gloves offered some grip and protection, but Ramirez wondered how Virgil was managing the climb below him in nothing but bare skin and sandals. The dead guide was nothing if not a mass of knowledge and secrets.

Ramirez was thankful for the difficulty of the climb. It kept his attention focused and his thoughts dormant. He felt robotic: Good grip, lower his body, find a foothold, find a second, repeat. It kept his feelings buried, which was good because none of the ones that pried at him would help in the slightest: Loss, Regret, Guilt—for his soldiers and for the home he'd likely never see again. When the thoughts boiled up he whispered his grandfather's prayer.

For the brief seconds those things crept into his mind, he imagined them buried deep within the ice of the Well. The only thought he kept was that of duty. The duty to reach the Center.

After what felt like hours, blue light filled the crevice and Virgil announced, "We are nearly there." Virgil's stoic voice was now somber as if the gravity of the place was affecting even him.

The blue light was overwhelming now, drowning out Ramirez's headlamp. At first he thought the light was coming from somewhere deep within it, deep underground, but now it was so powerful that it seemed like it was coming from the ice itself—from every curve, facet and crack.

The crevice opened up and the world was blue. The Well was a frozen lake surrounded by sheer walls of ice on all sides and capped with a blue grey sky that closed them in and cut them off from the Steps above. Even though it was the smallest Circle, the frozen surface still stretched to the horizon on all sides.

But it was finite. For the first time, Ramirez could see clear across the Circle to the other side and he knew that there was nothing left after this.

In the icy walls of the Well there were twisting forms beneath the ice, towering—titanic—some reaching even as far up as the dark clouds in the sky. They were contorted so that only portions of their humanoid bodies reached near the surface of the ice. Ramirez thought back to Virgil's comment about strange and mythical creatures and how some even lorded over their own slivers of Hell… but none ruled here. They were all frozen prisoners.

Ramirez stood, awestruck by the scene, all the while a sense of dread built within him. His stomach churned, his legs were stiff. His right hand clutched his rifle as if it would offer any protection against the elements or against whatever fate they found in the Center of the Well. His left hand tightly held his grandfather's cross and it felt as powerless as the rifle.

Sergeant Wilson stood beside him, breathing fast. "I guess this is it," he said quickly.

Hector Ramirez glanced at his second-in-command, his best friend and embraced him. Together, in the cold they recited Omega's creed. "I am an Omega Soldier. I will bravely go to places that don't exist and against beings that strike fear into the hearts of men. I am a beacon in the darkness and a bastion against the occult. My will is incorruptible and my body is my own. *Mi voluntad es incorruptible y mi cuerpo es mío.* Amen." It helped, if only a little. It might as well have been a candle in the darkness.

Virgil stepped out from the shelter of the cave wall and onto the ice, but even his steps were timid. Ramirez wanted to blame it on the ice, but the surface was coarse beneath his feet. Whatever moisture that clung to the walls further up was completely absent here.

Of the many fears that festered inside Ramirez, walking on the rough ice was not one of them.

The two soldiers followed Virgil out across the Well.

Ramirez lost track of time. He knew that walking to the center couldn't have been longer than the climb down the crevice or walking endless Hallway or across the Field, but walking to the center of the Well felt more immense than everything that came before.

They were close to the Center.

He could think of nothing but the building dread. The festering pit in his stomach that now crawled up the back of his neck. The three walked slowly across the coarse, cracked ice and Ramirez made the mistake of looking down.

Bodies were buried beneath the ice. Uncountable bodies. Some were close enough to the surface to see their twisted limbs and equally twisted faces, while others were specks of color deep beneath the ice.

For the first time since the crevice, Virgil spoke, "The ice is their punishment, for those here have forsaken warmth. They have forsaken the very ties that bind us together. The very ties that bind us to—"

A frigid wind blew across the lake causing all three of them to turn and cower from the biting cold. When it was over, Ramirez and Wilson were shaking.

Virgil stared at them wide-eyed and still. "Forgive me. The rest is not mine to say."

The guide led them the rest of the way to the Center. A spot marked by the dark, nearly black ice and the gravity of dread surrounding it.

When they were there, at the Center of the Well, Ramirez saw the dark ice for what it was: A shadow—no—a creature beneath the ice. The bulk of the shadow was from a single, massive, clawed hand, reaching for the surface. Unlike the giant humans frozen in the walls around them, the creature beneath the ice wasn't human. Even deeper down, two twisted black spires reached for the surface—horns. In the distant corners of Ramirez's vision, two massive bat-thin wingtips reached for the surface.

"That's of no concern to you," said a new voice from behind them.

Lieutenant Ramirez and Sergeant Wilson whipped around, rifles shouldered. Ramirez's heart was pounding in his ears.

The man stood only two yards away from them on the ice. The suddenness of his appearance and sight of him was overwhelming. He wore a long white cloak adorned with golden braids, but the white surface shimmered as if gold was woven into the sheer fibers.

He towered shoulders over the soldiers and Virgil—easily seven feet tall. In spite of his frame, his face was thin and nearly effeminate. His skin was olive and flawless. His hair was long, dark and pulled back with a golden crown.

Of all the many things unsettling about Lucifer, the worst was his demeanor. He did not talk with the bearing of a devil or a lord. The fallen archangel spoke with a carefree tone. He smiled warmly, like a friend you had seen yesterday.

The most terrifying thing about the Devil was that Hector Ramirez was not surprised by anything about him: Hector was not surprised to see Lucifer there; he had known what lay at the Center of the Well. He was not surprised at the subtleness of the Devil's appearance, for Lucifer was the thing by which all creeping, subtle, and patient things were measured. He was not surprised at the form Lucifer took, no more than he was surprised at the way Atticus Wilson looked. Lucifer Lightbringer was, after all, the most beautiful, powerful angel, second only to God—and they were far from God's house.

No, Hector was not surprised by any of those things. Hector was only surprised at the suddenness of his appearance.

Hector felt that he had known Lucifer his whole life. Even more than he knew Sergeant Atticus Wilson.

"One of the greatest curses bestowed upon me was that of *Time*," Lucifer said. He walked slowly. His hands clasped behind his back as he paced idly around them—like a friend might do while they waited for the train.

"In Heaven, there is no such thing. All things that will happen, have happened. Heaven is a stasis. Unchanging. Perfect. If you searched long enough, you would find everyone in Heaven, even those destined for it that are not yet dead yet or still in the lower realms.

"I didn't know time until I fell into the Lake of Violence." He made a sweeping gesture from the sky to the lake for emphasis. "I punctured the world."

Hector followed his gesture back from the Well of ice up through the clouds, stretching his mind to try to understand the magnitude of that statement.

The Devil continued casually, "Hell is effervescent. It mirrors the chaos and change of *His* world above. Down here, I *wait* for things to happen. For certain events to transpire. For sins to be committed. But sometimes, just sometimes—I don't have to wait quite as long. For that, I thank you."

Hector's eyes grew wide. Somewhere buried within him was the question. One that he had taken for granted as they descended into Hell; as he had grown numb from pain and loss.

Every single one of his men had been trapped within a Circle except for Lieutenant Ramirez and Sergeant Wilson…

What Circle would they be trapped in? What had Hector Ramirez done—what sin had he committed?

Hector's voice was weak as he repeated Virgil's words. "There are no accidents in Hell. Everyone winds up where they are meant to be." His voice shook, "What have I done?"

Thoughts of Omega Squad—his men—bubbled up inside him. They walked through the Circles of Hell and perished in the Circles of Hell because of Ramirez's command. The pain and loss of each of his men was replaced with fear. Fear that grew, fear that exploded, in the back of his mind with violent nausea.

Hector Ramirez collapsed to his knees. Eyes closed. Shaking with indescribable, child-like, primal terror.

Even Lucifer's soothing voice—the voice of a friend—was nothing in comparison.

"Of all the punishments in Hell, I find the ice of the Well most poetic," the Devil said. "You see, the gravest sin of all lies here, with me. It is a sin against the very warmth of life and Heaven. A sin against love. The ice is their punishment. They spend eternity devoid of the warmth and love they forsook. Trapped by ice, they can neither come together to reconcile or push away from those they wronged. They feel only cold.

"The greatest sin of all is *Betrayal.*"

As the words echoed across the ice, Ramirez felt he might sink into it. At any moment it might open up and swallow him. He would disappear into his rightful place as a traitor to his squad, to the men that trusted him with their lives. The men he marched into Hell, and continued to march even as he knew they would succumb one-by-one.

But the ice never opened. The ice never opened.

Hector finally opened his eyes and saw Lucifer pacing, exactly as he had the entire time. Ramirez looked to his best friend and to Virgil, both of whom he had forgotten about in his panic.

Atticus was beside him, pointing his rifle at Hector.

Virgil was several yards away from all of them, watching.

"I'm sorry," Hector said. His voice came out in a croak. "I'm sorry." He would've apologized for each and every man if he thought he could manage so without breaking. Or if he thought it would make a difference.

Hector Ramirez waited in tense silence for judgement of his sins that never came. All the while he stared down the barrel of his best friend's rifle.

"Come now, Hector," Lucifer said calmly. "I made an exception for you. You were just following orders. That lands you somewhere within the bowels of Hell, but not here. I *allowed* you to come this far because you brought him. *I wanted Sergeant Atticus Wilson.*"

In confusion, Hector turned from his friend, to the Devil. "I—I don't understand. He's been nothing but good to me. At the Lake of Fire he was going to leave us, after… But he didn't leave. Atticus is with me."

With immortal calm, Lucifer replied, "It's not about what Atticus was going to do. It's about what he *did*."

Hector turned back to his friend in confusion. Atticus was still pointing his rifle at Hector. He was quivering. His eyes glistened with tears.

"Hector… I—God, I'm so sorry. I'm so, so sorry. Tracey and I… We…" he trailed off.

Quiet as a predator, Lucifer walked over and stood just over Atticus's shoulder. He leaned down and whispered in his ear.

"Go on. Confess to him like your life depends on it."

Meanwhile, Hector was still on his knees, staring at the Devil and his best friend.

"Christ. We… We kissed on New Year's. You were already asleep. It should've stopped there, but it didn't. Two years… Each time the squad came home, Tracey and I would see each other. God, Hector, I'm so sorry. We were both lonely—"

"Lonely?" Hector muttered. "*My wife* was lonely? What the fuck is that supposed to mean?"

Atticus looked down at the ice. The barrel of the rifle drooped.

"Tell him," Lucifer whispered in his ear.

"She's going to leave you," Atticus finally said, meeting his eyes again. "She wasn't—she isn't happy." His face was sincere.

Hector didn't want to believe it, but then his mind drifted back. Back to the Hallway. Back to Not-Tracey, the demon that looked like his wife. She had stared at Atticus as Omega Squad passed. Hector hadn't wanted to believe it at the time, he had pushed the thought away and forgotten about it, but Not-Tracey had been staring at Atticus. His best friend had lusted after his wife, but it had grown, it had festered into something sinister, something cold.

Hector couldn't move from the ice. His gut was a mix of disgust and anger, caught between wanting to retch and wanting to throttle his best friend. The emotions sloshed within him until they finally dropped out from under him, like someone had pulled out the drain plug from somewhere inside him.

His wife was going to leave him… Tracey and his daughter, Anna, would leave him. But the hurt stretched even further. For two years his wife and his best friend had betrayed him. Two years they kept up the ruse. Did she even love him anymore? When had she stopped loving him? Why?

Why didn't his wife love him anymore?

Hector Ramirez felt hollow, like his heart had been ripped out, but the tiny fist-sized organ had torn out so much more with it. The hole inside him had opened up wider than the Well, the Chasm, or even the Lake and felt like it would stretch to the edge of Hell. A cataclysmic emptiness had opened inside of him.

And when Hector thought he was at the edge, when the void inside him had grown beyond incomprehensible, Atticus pulled the trigger.

~ ~ ~

The Hollows

The gunshot brought Hector back to the moment. The sound rang out and echoed through the void. For a moment, the sound filled him and it was all he knew.

He fell over from his knees and lay on his back on the ice. The Lieutenant should've felt pain, but he felt nothing. He ran gloved hands over his vest and chest plate, then over his arms and legs. Hector hadn't been shot.

Hector turned and looked at his friend, fearing the worst. Fearing that Atticus had taken his own life—

—But Sergeant Atticus Wilson stood, just as he had. Rifle barrel pointed at his best friend—at Hector. Atticus was shaking. His eyes were wide in horror. Whether it was in horror at what he had done or what hadn't happened, Hector could only guess.

Maybe the same hollow feeling had opened inside of his best friend.

The Devil still stood behind Atticus. The beautiful fallen angel no longer leaned in close and whispered. He towered over the Sergeant. "Now, now, Atticus. Haven't you already done enough?"

Lucifer draped a silk-laden arm around Atticus's shoulder and neck and the soldier wept. Then they floated or glided across the ice, the Devil effortlessly dragging his quarry. Atticus's cries for help receded into the distance. Hector reached for him, pawing silently.

Across the Well, Lucifer unceremoniously cast Hector's best friend down into the ice. The ice didn't so much as move or crack. It was like he had phased through it or as if there had always been a spot there for Atticus Wilson.

Then Lucifer glided back across the ice and stopped a yard from Hector Ramirez. He stood and stared at Hector, and even though Hector felt impossibly far away, somewhere deep within the unfathomable void that had opened in the pit of his stomach, the Devil saw him clearly.

Hector pushed himself to his feet and the Devil waited. "What happens now?" Despite *who* Hector was talking to, the emptiness inside him kept his voice from shaking.

Lucifer smiled warmly, "Now you go back."

Hector turned and looked back across the ice, possibly toward the crevice he climbed down. Then he looked up into the grey sky above the Well and tried to imagine the journey back the way he came. It would've been an impossible task had he not already been inside his own emptiness… now the task felt ludicrous. Laughable.

"No," Lucifer said. "You will go through the Hollows. Go back home."

Hector looked at the Devil in confusion. "I don't understand."

"You brought me a fitting prize, Hector, but you were just following orders. Everything you did in the military was at the command of someone else. Everything you did here was under the orders of someone else. Your commander, Staging Area Alpha and Bravo.

"Everything you did in life was at the beckon of someone else. Your parents, your wife. You lack ambition, you lack desire. You let others choose for you.

"Do you know why the pitiful creatures before the river Acheron reached out to you? Because that is where you belong. You belong with the indecisive, with the angels who took no sides and with the people who lived for nothing. You were as powerless here as you have been your entire life."

The Devil said these things warmly, without malice and the words should've devastated him, but they didn't. Hector Ramirez heard the words of the Devil, but he was already empty and numb.

"What was the point?"

"Making it to the Center was never your mission. Your mission was merely to make it to each Staging Area and receive further direction. You were told to come here and now *I* am giving you further direction: Go home, Hector. Virgil will escort you."

Hector turned and saw the stoic guide standing across the ice. He had forgotten Virgil was there. He hadn't moved at all.

When Hector turned back, the Devil was gone. Ramirez and Virgil were alone on the ice.

The broken Lieutenant walked across the ice to his lone companion. "How am I supposed to go home?" he wondered aloud. How was he supposed to go home to Tracey and Anna, knowing what he did?

But Hector followed his guide across the ice. Pushed on by his last set of orders. Devoid of his own directive.

Virgil didn't console him with answers. He merely walked beside Hector.

Virgil led Hector Ramirez to the Hollows, another crevice in the icy wall of the Well. Instead of going up, this one went horizontal. The blue glow of the ice receded and gave way to rock and stone. Darkness never came.

From somewhere up ahead, somewhere distant, light filtered through the crevice.

Soon the crevice was wide enough for the two men to walk beside one another and grew wider still until they were walking beside a thin, bubbling stream.

"The Hollows are different for everyone that passes through, but the River of Forgetfulness is the same," Virgil said.

Hector laughed. It was a hoarse and absurd sound. "Is that really its name?"

Virgil shrugged. "I did not come up with it. Sometimes simpler is better."

"What will I forget?"

The guide shook his head. "You will forget very little. You will remember the pain, but it will lessen. The chasm will shrink, if only a little."

Virgil spoke as if they came from a place of understanding, of having felt pain and loss the depths of which might even have rivaled Hector's. Ramirez looked at his guide and realized just how little he knew of the man, or spirit.

Virgil continued, "The River of Forgetfulness is not for the pain. It is so you do not remember the Hollows. So you do not remember the way out of Hell.

"You will not know how far you have walked or how much time has passed, but one day you will be through the Hollows. You will find yourself standing in a field with the sun on your face, wondering how you could have possibly made it through all that you have suffered, all that you have seen and felt and lived.

"But you will have made it, all the same."

~ ~ ~

Epilogue

Report: Mission **[Redacted]**

Reports would say that Omega Squad passed through the portal and made contact with Staging Area Alpha.

Reports would say that Lieutenant Hector Ramirez and the guide, **[Name Redacted],** emerged from the portal located in **[Location Redacted]**. The other **[Number Redacted]** members of **[Name Redacted]** and translators Dr. David Levy and Dr. Nancy Reed were killed in action.

Lieutenant Ramirez claimed to have made contact with Staging Area Bravo after heavy casualties. All other attempts to contact Staging Area Bravo have failed, so Lieutenant Ramirez's story could not be confirmed. The status of Staging Area Bravo is logged as unknown.

The two somehow returned to Home Base without making second contact with Staging Area Alpha. Neither the Lieutenant nor **[Name Redacted]** could explain how they traversed through **[Name Redacted]** and back through a second means.

The Lieutenant's testimony as to the fates of his squad have been logged and will be disseminated as needed. Additional units will be brought in and briefed with this new information.

Next Objective: Reestablish contact with Staging Area Bravo.

Additional Objectives: Investigate and corroborate Lieutenant Ramirez's account. Locate the second means of entry to **[Location Redacted]**.

~ ~ ~

Lieutenant Hector Ramirez

For a long time after leaving Hell, Hector Ramirez thought of *Time*.

The Devil's words echoed in his head: That down in Hell he had to wait for things. That, in respect to Time, Hell mirrored the world above. Virgil's words echoed in his head as well: That one day he would make it out of the Hollows. He had passed through the cave, but didn't feel the warmth of the sun.

Hector had made it back to Home Base and through debriefing. He was being sent home.

Now he was on a C-130 cargo plane heading for the East Coast. Only a handful of other passengers were going back to the States. Only a handful of crates were going back. Ramirez chuckled with black humor that they all must have been discarded things like himself.

Most of the space on the plane was empty. Hollow.

He would layover and fly the rest of the way to the West Coast. But maybe not. Hector found himself in no hurry to return home. No—he had a pit in his stomach, dreading the return.

Maybe he would stay awhile.

The C-130 touched down and the loading ramp descended, slowly letting the evening sun fill the void. The air was cool. Ramirez had forgotten that it was Springtime on this side of the world.

Lieutenant Ramirez walked down the loading ramp and into the tarmac of an airport he didn't recognize. Off in the distance, ocean waves churned. Whatever airport he had been brought to, it was right on top of the ocean.

He turned and regarded the rest of the airport, which wasn't much. There might have been three runways and a single control tower. Beyond those was a dock that wrapped around the coast. Hundreds—thousands of people disembarked from ships.

Ramirez stared for a long while before he realized what was wrong with the picture. It wasn't the array of different ships. Some were military, some civilian. All from different time periods. Among them he saw a steamboat and one in the same style as the Titanic.

No—the strangest thing was that everyone disembarked without luggage. All those dots of people without a single box carried or dragging behind them.

Hector turned and followed the procession of travelers across the ports.

Just beyond the ports, a lone mountain rose up into the sky, past the clouds, and a city rose up on its sides. Buildings dotted the face of it and were divided by seven white walls that ringed all the way around the mountain. The first wall that ringed the foot of the mountain was only a mile or so away. A crowd gathered around it, so large that he could see it from a distance.

He stood there, staring at the ringed mountain and the procession, and knew that there was no such thing in the States. He was not on a military base because he saw only two other uniformed soldiers. Maybe they were laid over in a private airport in Europe. Ramirez had been in a haze when his travel route was discussed. He must have missed it.

Hector told himself those things until he saw Virgil standing beside him. The grey-robed guide smiled warmly. Ramirez didn't return his smile.

"I thought I was going home," Hector said absently.

"Not yet," Virgil replied. "Besides, you are not ready to go home."

Ramirez shrugged. "You're not wrong about that."

Virgil nodded. "We are in Ostia and you have a ways to go before you return home."

The pair stared at the sea of people gathered around the wall of the city and Hector Ramirez knew that Virgil spoke the truth. In spite of the mountain and the journey ahead of him, Hector felt the slightest touch of the sun on his face. He was no longer in Hell and Hector had a feeling that he was not back to the realm of the living. In spite of that, deep within him he kindled the light of hope.

The soldier fumbled his grandfather's cross, but somehow the words and prayers that used to come so easily did not. Finally, Hector said, "I can't find the words."

"Faith is *trust*. To have faith, is to not know what the outcome is going to be. You have to trust."

RAMIREZ'S STORY WILL CONTINUE IN

Across Purgatory

Thank you for Reading

I hope you enjoyed reading this story as much as I enjoyed writing it. If you did, I would greatly appreciate a short review on Amazon or your favorite book website. Reviews are crucial for any author, and even just a line or two can make a huge difference.

Looking for more Strange Places?

You might like **The Secret of Milton Boska**. It's a short story, but it might scratch that same itch.

There are no records of what's on asteroid Epsilon 2-B. No record of the containment facility. What lies a mile down, deep within its frozen confines?

Find out what terrifies Milton Boska.

If you're in the mood for an ongoing serial, check out **A Battleaxe and a Metal Arm**. I plan on including lots of strange, awe-inspiring and eerie locations in each one. It's got a little more action than Milton Boska, but no less strangeness.

A sorceress with a metal arm and a barbarian with a battle-axe stuck in an endless, changing dungeon. *Come for the action. Stay for the mystery.*

On writing
Descent into Hell

The genesis of a story is an interesting thing to me. What that story becomes over the course of writing it—now that's even more interesting.

The first iteration of *Descent into Hell* was simple enough: *Special Forces soldiers fighting their way through Hell.* It was one of the first story ideas I had back in my early 20's, when I was first starting to put some serious effort into writing. I didn't get far with it. I moved on to other things. There it stayed in a journal of ideas. Dormant. Waiting. I rediscovered it right before lockdowns happened in the U.S. and it was one of the stories I developed over that first "COVID year".

At some point it turned from simple military paranormal thriller into a reimagining of Dante's *Inferno*. I mapped out the different Circles and kept their order from the original story. I took liberties with most of the Circles, but some, such as The Pit and The Well are pretty close to the original source material, at least in physical description.

Coincidentally, what led me to doing a reimagining of Dante's *Inferno* was also what kept me away from doing a straight "retelling" of the story.

Early on, I imagined these soldiers getting picked off, one by one as they went deeper into Hell. Even then, I knew it would culminate with that ultimate sin, betrayal, at the center. That's what I wanted to focus on, rather than in the original epic poem where Dante focused on random historical figures that happened to be trapped in each Circle. I also knew I wanted to play up the horror and dread of each Circle and the fact that, at any time, they might succumb to that Circle's sin.

I also had an idea for continuing the story through Purgatory and Heaven, but it wasn't until I got to the end of Inferno and I was left with the broken lieutenant that I knew exactly *how* I would continue his story. The full trilogy, tentatively called *Omega Absolution*, is going to follow Hector Ramirez out of Hell, across Purgatory and into Heaven.

What to expect in the sequel: *Across Purgatory*

Normally, I would leave you hanging in suspense with what to expect in the next book, but in this case that's not quite fair. *Across Purgatory* is going to be a different book. In Dante's *Purgatorio*, the narrator and Vigil traverse the terraces of the mountain which is broken up into levels (much like Hell). Each focuses on a different virtue. Dante's *Paradiso* is much the same. I plan on following both in terms of the "ring structure" of each place. But that's where most of the similarities will end.

In the sequel to *Descent into Hell,* instead of horror and suspense, it is going to focus on Ramirez coming to terms with his wife and his best friend's infidelity. Rather than struggling through the horrors of Hell, he is going to struggle through accepting what happened. Each terrace and each virtue is going to represent a different aspect of his healing.

In short, I want you to know what you're signing up for with the rest of this series. If you came to *Descent* for the action and horror, you may not want to stay for the rest. That's okay. I'm all about reader expectations and I don't want you sitting around waiting for more horror and action when there won't be any more in the other two books in the trilogy. I'm grateful either way that you stuck around and I hope you enjoyed *Descent*. It can totally be read as a standalone story.

But if you're like me, then you won't be content with just knowing that Ramirez made it out of Hell. I thought *Descent* would be the end of the story. Once I was done, I realized that I needed to follow Ramirez's story the rest of the way. I needed to see him make it through Purgatory and through Heaven. As Virgil said, sometimes us mortals need to see to believe.

So, if you're interested in seeing the rest of Ramirez's story, then stay in touch. You can sign up for my mailing list and be the first to know when *Across Purgatory* is released.

Further Reading

If you're interested in reading the original Dante's *Inferno* (or the entire *Divine Comedy*) then you're in luck, because you can find it in the classics for section for free. It's quite a bit different than the story you just read, but it's great in its own right (a classic for a reason). If you find the poetry hard to parse, then you can look for abridged versions or even summaries to get you through it.

Connect with the Author

If you want to stay up to date on the latest about Samuel's publishing news and blog, check out his website and consider signing up for his monthly newsletter.

www.SamuelFlemingBooks.com

Samuel can also be found on Goodreads and Facebook.

Samuel Fleming is a Science Fiction and Fantasy author.

He grew up in Maryland, spending most of his time swimming and writing. Swimming gave him a lot of time to daydream, so the two hobbies complemented each other well. Idle day dreams turned into stories, some of which stuck with him for years. These days he swims a little less and writes a lot more.

He loves a good story no matter the medium: Books, TV, video games, comics, tabletop RPG's, or podcasts—most of which he attempts to share with his wife and three kids, and occasionally on his blog.

* 9 7 8 1 9 5 4 6 7 9 0 7 8 *